M
is
oth
loc
housework, reading and travelling.

Michael has written adult fiction and children's books, for which he has won several awards. His first children's book, *Titans!*, was shortlisted for the Children's Book Council Book of the Year Award for Younger Readers in 1993. His most recent, *Blat Magic*, won the Queensland Premier's Award for Best Children's Book in 2002. *Mudlark* was shortlisted for the Children's Book Council Award for Younger Readers in 2004.

'With writing so beautiful that you stop for a moment to admire it and a story so superbly crafted that it takes your breath away, this is a rare gem. Highly recommended.'

Good Reading magazine, September 2003

'*Mudlark* is a poetic, insightful, deeply human novel.'

Australian Book Review, March 2004

'... a beautifully written text, rich in metaphor and simile. Highly recommended.'

Reading Time, November 2003

Other Angus & Robertson books by
Michael Stephens

mudLARK

michael stephens

📚 Angus&Robertson
An imprint of HarperCollins*Publishers*

Angus&Robertson
An imprint of HarperCollins*Publishers*, Australia

First published in Australia in 2003
by HarperCollins*Publishers* Pty Limited
ABN 36 009 913 517
A member of the HarperCollins*Publishers* (Australia) Pty Limited Group
www.harpercollins.com.au

HarperCollins*Publishers*
25 Ryde Road, Pymble, Sydney NSW 2073, Australia
31 View Road, Glenfield, Auckland 10, New Zealand
77–85 Fulham Palace Road, London W6 8JB, United Kingdom
2 Bloor Street East, 20th floor, Toronto, Ontario M4W 1A8, Canada
10 East 53rd Street, New York NY 10022, USA

National Library of Australia Cataloguing-in-publication data:

Stephens, Michael, 1955– .
    Mudlark.
    Children aged 11 to 14.
    ISBN 0 207 19980 9.
    1. Children and death – Juvenile fiction. I. Title.
A823.3

Cover and internal designed by Christa Edmonds, HarperCollins Design Studio
Typeset in 11/15 Berkeley Book by HarperCollins Design Studio
Printed and bound in Australia by Griffin Press on 60gsm Bulky Paperback

5 4 3 2   04 05 06

PART ONE

PART ONE

'You there! Yes, you, the boy running. Come here.
Now catch your breath. A few nice, deep breaths,
please. In through the nose and out through the
mouth.'

The new deputy-headmaster's tie gleamed in the
morning sunlight. Mr Harding's voice was loud and
deep, yet he was the smallest teacher in the school,
shorter than some of the Year Six boys. From
weekends spent sailing, his skin was tanned golden
brown.

Boys were streaming across the playground. By lunchtime the asphalt would be as soft as the low-tide mud at the Creek, and the teacher on duty would tell everyone to stay in covered, shadowy places.

'What's your name?' asked the deputy-headmaster.

'Jim Liddell.'

'Class?'

'Mr Bennet's.'

'You're very pale. Are you feeling well, Jim?'

'Yes, I am.'

The boy was used to this question. Small for twelve, and with skin that seemed paler than it was because of dark hair and eyes, he had told others:

'It's because my mother's family comes from Iceland. Everyone has snow-white skin there, and usually white hair too. They even drive white cars. Hides them from bears and wolves.'

Something about the way Mr Harding was rocking back on his heels, then tilting forward, meant that he had more to say.

'Jim Liddell, do your parents allow you come to school looking like this? Your socks, for a start. One grey and short, other long and black. And your shoes. I wonder if they have ever, in their whole lives, been polished? Please, don't interrupt. And your shorts are filthy. There seems to be paint on them. Look, beside the pocket. Green paint, if I'm not mistaken. And your shirt isn't tucked in. Hasn't been ironed, either. Plus, Jim, you need a haircut. Show me your hands please.'

Mr Harding expanded his nostrils like a dragon preparing to breathe fire.

'As I suspected. Dirty fingernails. So tell me, do your parents allow you to come to school like this?'

Jim gazed back at the gleaming tie.

Fewer boys were running across the asphalt now. Any second, the bell would go and classes would start. The morning had that fresh coolness that comes at the start of a really hot day. On Thursday of next week the summer holidays would begin.

'Mr Harding, my parents are dead. Both of them. So unless they see it from Heaven, they can't know that I come to school looking like this.'

Jim noticed droplets of sweat on the deputy-headmaster's upper lip.

'Dead?'

'Yes.' Jim widened his dark eyes ever so slightly.

'I see. I'm very sorry. I'm sorry that I asked that question. Plenty of boys failed to show the Newsletter with the uniform requirements to their parents. I was just … Anyway, I'm new here, as you know. Hurry then, to your class. If you're late, tell Mr Bennet that you were talking to me.'

Soft, summery air in his face, Jim ran across the soon-to-be-molten playground, defiantly breathing deeply in through his mouth and out through his mouth, only halting when he reached the shadow of the classroom block. Here he recalled Mr Harding's softer voice at the end of their conversation, and this reminded him of what a lonely thing it was to have both parents dead.

'How is your mother?' Sam Garrard asked as soon as Jim had slid behind his desk right at the back of Mr Bennet's class.

'Okay. All better. She got back yesterday. Still in bed, but she'll be up by Monday, she says.'

Jim closed his eyes and laid his head sideways on the desk. Sam was speaking, but Jim couldn't make out the words through the knocks and echoes that sounded as if they came not just through the desk, but from deep beneath the surface of the Earth.

Sam lived in Jim's street — Faraday Avenue, Tacker Bay — three houses closer to the golf-course.

Jim opened his eyes. The backs of Sam's hands were crowded with freckles, like his face. His hair was orange, perfectly straight, and long enough to cover his eyes when he leant forward. He dropped his desk-lid. The noise shocked Jim into sitting up.

Mr Bennet was pulling down the window to make it open at the top. The crescent-shaped flowers of a poinsettia tree shone a brighter red once they were no longer pressed against the glass.

Boys had their Geography exercise books out. Mr Bennet wrote the word 'Savanna' on the blackboard. Jim sat with his head in his hands, and his eyes widened as he gazed at the bird in a cage on its own little table between the teacher's desk and the open window.

The bird was called Mudlark, which was also the name of his species. Small even for a mudlark, in fact hardly bigger than a sparrow, he was black with a few white feathers. If he hadn't been in a cage he would have been making a nest from mud and twigs. Or at least he would have been doing this if the other mudlarks in Tacker Bay would agree not to attack him.

'A powerful storm, maybe a hurricane, carried Mudlark off-course,' Mr Bennet had explained to the class at the start of the year. 'Carried him too far from his normal flight-paths for him to be able to find his way back home again. And so he arrived in Tacker Bay, where none of the mudlarks know him, and where they feared that he might be a scout for an enemy flock. When I found him he had a broken wing and a cut on his head, and I knew that he wouldn't survive another day in Tacker Bay outside a cage. If ever I find out where his home is, I will take him there, and set him free. But that is not likely.'

Jim got his things out of his bag, including an exercise book with JOURNAL printed on the front.

Corners worn into softness, down the middle of its cover it had a fold that was nearly a tear.

As Sam copied the writing on the blackboard, Jim opened the Journal, flipped past page after page of words closely written in a patchwork of pencil and differently coloured inks, and wrote at high speed:

Mudlark had no parents. None. Both died soon after he was born. That was one of the main reasons he was chosen for such a dangerous mission. No-one at home would miss him if he failed to return.

He pushed the book back into his pack.

Mudlark gazed at the children before him. Eyes round and dark and wise, he tilted his head, thinking deep thoughts.

The cage was the largest they sold at Tacker Bay Pet Supplies. Made of wire painted white, it had a curved roof and, in bird terms, was three storeys high. Mudlark flew rather than merely jumped from perch to perch. He could check his reflection in a mirror, or ring a bell by pushing it with his beak. Bowls for seed and water were kept permanently full.

Peering straight down and darting his head from side to side, Mudlark often appeared to be reading the newspaper at the bottom of his cage.

Jim's chest and throat suddenly tightened with fear. Instead of thinking, he breathed deeply, closed his eyes, and soon began to feel almost normal again.

After lunch, with the morning freshness so lost that you couldn't believe it had ever existed, Mr Bennet stood beside Mudlark.

'And now,' he began, forehead glistening and wet patches at the armpits of his shirt, 'now is the time for deciding who will take Mudlark home for the weekend. I know I say it every week, but I'll say it again: it can't be anyone with a cat in the family. Mudlark is safe in his cage, I know, but birds have been known to die of fright when faced with the stare of a particularly fierce and patient cat.'

Boys already had their arms bent, ready to raise them.

'And this is both the last weekend of the term and of the whole school year. Next year you'll be in high school, and Mudlark won't be in your class any longer. So I only want those of you who haven't once, not even once, taken Mudlark home, to put up your hands.

'Okay. Those who haven't taken Mudlark home all year, and whose parents have agreed, please put up your hand.'

Amid accusations, hissed at first and then shouted, hands went up.

'You definitely took him home last term!' Thomas Lagoni accused Leo Playford.

'What about you?' Leo shouted. 'You've had him twice! *Twice!*'

'And you —'

'Hand down, liar!'

'I never —'

'Oh yes you —'

'Wait ... wait ... wait ... wait.' Soothingly, in time to his words, Mr Bennet pushed out his hands. 'Please. Be quiet. Now ...'

Like nearly everyone, Jim had his hand up. Yet although he had never taken Mudlark home, the fear that he had felt this morning now rushed back, and whispered:

You have no chance.

For although Mr Bennet had never exactly said so, getting to take Mudlark home was a reward for good behaviour. If you did well in a test, or better than usual, or at least didn't get into trouble, you had a hope of getting Mudlark.

But Jim was sometimes in trouble, and rarely, at least lately, did well in tests.

He would never get to take Mudlark home.

'Good luck,' whispered Sam, who'd had the bird only the weekend before last, as well as once in first term.

Sam had kept Mudlark in his bedroom. During the night, he claimed, the bird had *spoken* to him.

' "*I am a thinker,*" I thought he said,' Sam confided when Jim had come over on the Saturday morning. 'It was late. I was falling asleep. He spoke in a whispering voice, like sheets of paper scraping together. "*I am a thinker, so I do not mind being alone.*" Then he said: "*But there are some subjects it is better not to think about, just as there are some sights it is better not to see.*" And that's all he said.'

So Jim held his right arm up as straight and as high as he possibly could, and looked not at Mr Bennet, but at Mudlark, the bird from a distant place that he would never take home.

So when Mr Bennet said, 'Jim, Jim Liddell?' he wondered at first who this lucky boy was, and started to feel jealous.

Even when he realised that it was him, he feared that he might have fallen into what his mother called 'one of your dazes', and that the question of who was going to take Mudlark home had been settled long ago, and Mr Bennet was about to ask why he still had his hand up.

'Would you like to take Mudlark home this weekend, Jim?'

Mr Bennet had advanced halfway down the classroom. He had taken off his tie and undone the top button of his shirt. From the hollow of his throat curled three or four black hairs.

'Me?'

'Yes, Jim. You haven't taken Mudlark home this year, have you?'

'No, I haven't.'

'You don't have a cat, do you?'

'No, I don't.' And he added, although it sounded stupid even as he spoke, 'I don't have a dog either.'

'Good. Settled then. You take Mudlark home this weekend. The last weekend of the year.'

Amid sighs of disappointment, and some giggles at the irrelevance of Jim's confession that he didn't have a dog, Mr Bennet returned to the front of the class. And as everyone took out their Maths books, the classroom returned to normal for all except Jim.

Sam had his hand around his friend's arm.

'Did you hear that? It's you! *You!*'

'Yes.'

But Jim had just seen Mr Harding, the new deputy-headmaster, at the door of the classroom.

When he'd heard what Mr Harding had to say,

Mr Bennet would surely change his mind about who was going to take Mudlark home.

Mr Harding started talking to Mr Bennet. Both teachers glanced at Jim.

'What's wrong?' whispered Sam.

'Nothing.'

'Did you do something?'

'Probably.' Jim closed his eyes, refusing to remember the exact details of what he had told Mr Harding this morning.

The fear returned. Momentarily, Jim was certain that something had gone badly wrong with the whole world. Something far, far worse than not being able to take Mudlark home. If he tried, really tried, he might be able to work out what it was.

But he didn't want to.

Then Mr Harding left, and Mr Bennet started to teach as though nothing had happened.

So it hadn't been about him.

It hadn't.

The fear hadn't been caused by anything real, then. Just his fear of not getting, then of losing, Mudlark.

He laid his forehead on the desk, exhausted.

Then he took out his Journal and, hand cupped secretively around the pen-tip, wrote:

The whole world will one day have a last Friday. Or: the boy and the talking bird will find a way out of the castle — through the forest — to where a wizard lives who will stop the End of Time.

As he closed the book he noticed afternoon sunlight across Mr Bennet's desk. It struck a vase of daisies that Jim had not noticed before. Mostly in shadow now, the poinsettia flowers glowed like embers in a fire that is about to go out.

2

'I'm not just going to sit Mudlark on the desk in my room all weekend,' Jim told Sam as he stepped watchfully from the six-inch-high wall that separated the Shell Service Station from the footpath in New South Head Road, Tacker Bay.

Mudlark hopped from the middle to the upper perch as water sloshed from the bowl onto the cage's paper floor.

'No,' Jim went on, arm starting to ache from

holding the cage out to keep it from bumping into his leg. 'I'm going to inspire him to speak.'

Sam nodded at the other side of Old South Head Road.

'Look. Waddell and Sandra.'

As far as Jim knew, Andrew Waddell always spoke to boys smaller than himself with contempt. His shoulders were broad, legs thick with muscles. He went to St Xavier's in Dover Heights, which had broken up for the holidays a whole week ago.

Sandra Brownscombe lived opposite Jim, in a white house behind a white picket fence. Her father was completely bald, and washed his stationwagon every Sunday morning, except when it was raining, at precisely half-past ten. Jim thought Sandra beautiful, though he would never have told Sam or anyone else this. He had given her several made-up names in his Journal, never her real one. For weeks now she and Waddell had been hanging around together. Yet even with Andrew, she held her head high, and her nose had an upward tilt, and it was clear to Jim that in her own mind she was somewhere else. She wore her deep brown hair pulled back from her face in a ponytail bound around with a plain old rubberband.

He had written in his Journal:

She writes a Journal. I'm in it, but she doesn't write my name either.

'What about Behemoth?' Sam asked.

They had passed the TV repair shop. Waddell and Sandra were behind them, still on the opposite side of the road. Close together, shoulders almost touching, though not holding hands.

'Maybe in the holidays then,' Sam replied to Jim's silence.

He was accustomed to his friend's moods.

'What?'

'Nothing.'

'No, you were saying about Behemoth. Yes, not while I've got Mudlark. We'll trap Behemoth in the holidays.'

One Saturday night a few weeks ago, walking past the golf-course, they had heard a growling out of the darkness beyond the rusty old fence, a deep rumbling that could only have come from a savage and perhaps unknown species of beast. And since then they had imagined — or Jim had, with Sam happy to go along — that a monster, or behemoth, lived in the dense jungle there, and only came out when it was dark. Without admitting that it was genuine fear that caused them to do so, they had put off the time when, in the dead of night, they would crawl beneath the fence and seek out this monster.

Yet Jim was certain that one day he really would enter the golf-course and face Behemoth. For sometimes, just before he fell asleep, he imagined shadows in the golf-course curling around, like ink in water. And this darkness would creep across Newcastle Street, and down Faraday Avenue, to his own house, Number Nine.

At the corner of Faraday Avenue, a large dog of no particular breed, whose hair had once been black mottled with brown, but was now mostly grey, grinned at the boys.

'Hello Prince.' Jim was careful to keep Mudlark behind his back in case the sight of all those teeth, even if they were yellow and blunt with age, frightened the bird.

Mr Stevens, Prince's owner, was in his front yard carefully pouring water from a bucket into a ditch beside a bed of poppies. He was old, and had pure white hair. He called out:

'Jim! How's your mother getting along?'

'She's fine, Mr Stevens. Got home from hospital yesterday afternoon.'

'Good, good. Well, please give her my best wishes.'

'I'll come over and see Mudlark tomorrow,' Sam called out, waving goodbye at Jim's house.

Jim climbed the steps by the driveway, to the paving stones that his father had laid in the days when there had been no lawn, only mud with seeds in it and a sprinkler whirling around. Up the steps to the verandah with its concrete floor painted deep red, to the heavy door that had been solid glass until the day, about a year ago, when Jim had pushed at it with both hands in the belief that it was off the latch, and had plunged straight through. He had been running away from Andrew Waddell.

He hadn't felt a thing, until his mother sat him down in the kitchen and he saw both his legs and left arm glistening red. Only two of the cuts had been serious, and needed stitching. The others were mere scratches. Both scars were on his left side, one on the arm and one on the leg.

The front door opened onto a dark and chilly hallway. To the right was his parents' bedroom, where his mother was probably asleep.

He carried Mudlark down the hall, across a large room with a fireplace and rugs, into another hall. And now he knew that Paulie was home, because he could hear — as though from several houses away — a tune being played on a trumpet. Not in a jerky, practising way, but faultlessly, and with such feeling that you had to stop and listen.

After a long minute or so, Jim moved on past Paulie's door to his bedroom at the end. Here he placed Mudlark on a desk that had a plastic map of the world for its top. He pulled out the chair and sat facing the bird.

'Hello Mudlark. Home at last.'

The bird returned Jim's gaze, then darted his dark eyes around.

'You're happy, aren't you Mudlark? Do you know what? I am too. I don't think I've ever been happier in my whole life than at this moment right now.'

Mudlark in his room, where he would stay for the whole weekend. Tonight he would turn out the light and they would have a conversation.

Jim lay back on his bed, and after a few seconds of telling himself that he had never been happier than right now, realised that he was hungry.

Yet he remained where he was a moment longer. After all, it was Friday, after school. The long holidays began on Thursday of next week. Mudlark was on his desk.

He couldn't help it. He jumped up, knocked at Paulie's door, turned the handle and pushed it slightly open.

A few inches was all it would go, because of the foam mattress over it, positioned to block out the sound.

As Paulie dragged the mattress aside, the sudden brightness of the light forced Jim to narrow his eyes.

'What do you want?' Paulie asked coldly, not liking to be interrupted at his practising. The gold rims of his spectacles glinted, as did the keys of the trumpet held tightly by his side.

'I'm sorry, Paulie. You were playing such great music. I was going to ask you if you wanted something to eat. I'm getting something, and …'

Jim took a step forward, and his face lit up. Obviously, he was about to give the real reason for his visit.

'You know that bird in Mr Bennet's classroom, the one everyone gets to take home except for me?'

'Yes?'

'Well, I've got him for the weekend, Paulie. He's on my desk, if you want to take a look. And do you want' — this as Paulie slid the mattress further from

the door, and began to follow Jim into his room —
'and do you want something to eat, or drink?'

'No thanks. I had something on my way home.
Oh, there it is. Hello, bird. Can it sing?'

As usual, Paulie was interested only in the musical
possibilities.

'Yes, sometimes.'

'Will you get me, if he starts? And there isn't much
in the kitchen, Jim. Dad'll be going out for something
later, if you can wait till then. Or you can get
something from the shops. Do you have any money?'

'Yes, thank you, Paulie.'

His brother was only three years older, but
sometimes Jim felt as if he were talking to an adult,
or to someone even older — perhaps a white-haired
grandfather like Mr Stevens.

As Paulie closed his door and began to slide the
mattress back into place, Jim re-entered the room
containing the rugs and fireplace, and passed double
glass doors that opened onto the backyard.

The kitchen was dark, and like the rest of the
house was chilly on the afternoons of even hot days.

On the round dining-table was a pile of history books. The top one was *A History of the War of the Roses*. Shortly before getting sick, his mother had begun to study at the university. Now she must have asked for more books to read, while in bed getting better.

When his mother was well enough to leave her room, he would come and read with her, talk with her, whenever he wanted.

Jim halted.

Should he take Mudlark to his mother's room, to show her?

No, she was probably sleeping

He opened the fridge door. A piece of cheese in clingwrap was half green and half deep yellow. Jim sniffed the milk carton, jerked his head away, and put it straight back.

Nothing but half a packet of peas in the freezer. No bread. Biscuit jar empty except for crumbs.

It had been like this ever since his mother had gone into hospital.

He could go to the shops in Old South Head Road

for hot chips and a can of drink, but he didn't like the thought of leaving Mudlark alone.

Beside the sink was a mountain of family-sized pizza cartons. Jim raised the topmost one a fraction, to gauge by its weight if a slice had been left inside.

He was about to try the one underneath, which would only have been a day older, when the row of white boxes on top of the cupboards caught his eye. Even before Mum had gone into hospital, Dad had returned from the supermarket with the car full of toilet rolls and these cartons of cornflakes.

'Now we've taken care of the two most important things,' he had said. 'Breakfast and toilet.'

Joe found a bowl that wasn't too dirty, ran water around it to make it a fraction cleaner, poured cornflakes in, and raced from the kitchen.

'Want one?' he asked Mudlark, poking a flake between the bars of the cage while pushing a handful into his own mouth.

The bird tilted his head as though to say, '*Most considerate of you, Jim.*' He hopped closer, touched the cornflake with the tip of his beak, then flew to the topmost perch and gazed at the window.

Delicate, pepper-tree leaves brushed the glass.

Up close to the cage, Jim found himself seeing the world through bars.

'Oh Mudlark.' He sighed. 'Wouldn't you like to be free, even for a minute? Perhaps you'd like to fly around my room?'

The cage door was the sort that simply slides up. No lock or catch.

Mudlark was tame. He had come close enough to a human hand, hadn't he, to taste the cornflake? If I let him out, Jim reasoned, he'll fly around this room, have fun, and when he's tired I'll put him back inside. And I'll tell Mr Bennet, and some day if everyone agrees to stay still and silent, he'll let out Mudlark to become truly a part of the class instead of just a bird in a cage.

Then, perhaps, Mudlark would learn things, and have his own desk. And it wouldn't be long before he picked up a pen or pencil in his beak, or using his wings, and wrote. And in no time he'd be a proper member of the class, and like a human would progress through the grades until eventually he would graduate from school, having learnt enough to decide where he wanted to live and what he wanted to do.

Jim pulled his Journal and pen from his bag.

Mudlark spoke for the first time shortly after morning break on the first Monday of second term. No-one but J could believe their ears. His words were: 'I thank you all for being so kind to me.'

3

Jim went to close his door, paused to listen to Paulie's distant-sounding, lovely trumpeting, then heard a clanking from the backyard, followed by glass shattering.

From Mrs Hogan's place, he realised. Opening a door opposite Paulie's, he stepped straight out onto a courtyard made of hand-sized stones set into concrete.

To his right were the glass doors at the back of the house. Opposite was the laundry. Beyond the courtyard, to his left, was the backyard. A shadow had fallen across the grass, just short of the end.

'Damn and blast you, stubborn objects!' came an old woman's raspy voice.

Feet on the crossbar of the fence, Jim peered over.

Mrs Hogan was bent double, picking up shards of broken glass and putting them into a plastic bin.

'Ah Jim.' Straightening, she shook her head sadly. 'Here I am, always in some mess or other. These bags are so flimsy. You simply can't trust them. Not for a second. But no, I don't mind. Not at all. Disasters give me an excuse to stay outside and listen to your brother's wonderful trumpet-playing.'

The music was louder here, since Paulie didn't have a mattress over his window, and had even left it open a few inches at the top.

'I'm your brother's biggest fan.' She raised a broken bottle-neck, index finger inside it, and watched its sharp edges sparkle on their way to the bin. 'But he told me that he intends never to give a performance, not a single one in his whole life. Is that true, Jim? Tell me it isn't true.'

She let go of the glass and looked directly at him.

Her face was covered with wrinkles, and she wore bifocals that magnified the skin beneath her eyes, while leaving the eyelids and eyes themselves normal-sized. It seemed to Jim that not only had she lived next door all his life, but that she had remained through all that time exactly as ancient as she was now.

Occasionally Mrs Hogan sang out loud, either alone or to accompany Paulie on his trumpet. One night Sam had been over to stay, and when Mrs Hogan started singing he had said:

'My father says she's an alcoholic, but my mother says that she's mad, but harmless. My sister thinks she's a witch.'

Jim had said nothing. He had been shocked to discover that others knew about Mrs Hogan.

'Is she?' he had asked his mother the next day, over breakfast. 'Is Mrs Hogan an alcoholic or mad? Or a witch?'

His mother's voice was deeper than that of any woman he knew, and people said that her eyes were just like his.

'No, I've spoken to Mrs Hogan. She's a clever woman. No, brilliant. And I'm afraid that no-one, no-one at all, is capable of judging her. To my mind she's a kind of Empress.'

Sometimes, especially when angry or indignant, his mother said strange things. But Jim had no doubt that they were true.

'And you, Jim,' Mrs Hogan asked, kicking the last few glittering fragments of glass into the bushes, 'what have you been up to? How are things?'

'I'll show you. Just a sec.' He ran back to his room, picked up the cage and returned to Mrs Hogan. One elbow over the fence, standing on the crossbar, he lifted it up.

Mrs Hogan straightened her glasses. 'Why, a mudlark. What's your name, darling?'

'Mudlark,' Jim answered.

'Can he talk? Some of them do, you know.'

And before Jim could answer, Mrs Hogan went on, reflectively:

'I had a kitten once, who could. Eloise, I called her. Ran away. Never —'

'He can,' Jim interrupted, balancing the cage on the fence as water slopped from the bowl and Mudlark dashed to the top perch. 'You know Sam, Sam-three-doors-down, well, he had him a few weeks ago and he says that Mudlark spoke to him during the night.'

Mrs Hogan nodded as though she had expected to hear this.

'I well remember,' she continued, 'the first time Eloise spoke to me. I was chopping up vegetables, and she hopped onto the bench. Which strictly speaking she wasn't supposed to do. And she said as clearly as I'm talking to you now, "Watch out that you don't hurt yourself. You're bringing that knife much too close to your fingertips." '

Like the broken glass, Mrs Hogan's eyes sparkled.

'An expression of concern such as that takes you by surprise. Especially after you've lived alone for a bit. After that we had some lovely chats, she and I. But listen to that heavenly music of your brother's! Makes me want to cry, sometimes, from sheer pleasure. And what's that, Jim? Isn't someone calling you? Your father? Well, I'll be seeing you. Take care.'

'Jim?' came his father's call.

'Coming!'

'What's that?' Mr Liddell was stepping onto the courtyard.

He was a tall man, and so thin that his shirts and trousers couldn't help looking too big for him. He brushed his thinning, dark hair straight back from his forehead, and went on before Jim could answer, 'Where did you get the bird?'

When Jim had explained, his father blinked at Mudlark for a moment longer, as though not quite understanding.

'I see. All right.' He followed Jim into his room, and watched him place the cage on the map of the world. A beam of sunlight stretched right across the South Pole.

For a few seconds they stood, listening to Paulie's music.

'Jim ...'

But just then a 'Hello!' came from the backyard, which meant that someone had come down the side path.

As Mr Liddell started for the door, Jim muttered quickly:

'It's okay. I've had something to eat. Do you want me to ring for pizza later?'

'What? Yes please.'

In the courtyard was Mick Ryan, from three houses past Mrs Hogan, carrying a clinking carton of brown bottles.

'Didn't knock at the front for fear of waking the patient,' he explained to Mr Liddell. 'Here, brought a little present for you.' Putting down the bottles of beer, he asked, 'How is she, Tony?'

'She's fine, Mick, and thank you very much for the beer.'

Mick Ryan's T-shirt smelt of soap powder, and was brilliantly white against the brown of his neck and arms.

Jim's parents had referred to Mick as 'retired', without ever specifying exactly what he had retired from. And although Jim had asked everyone he knew, no-one could say what it was that Mick Ryan had done.

Nowadays he made beer in a garage in his backyard, and brought around a carton of bottles every now and then. On some Saturday nights, before Jim's mother had got sick, she would spread a green blanket over the dining table, and Mick and Mrs Griswold, from Mr Liddell's office, would come and play cards.

While Mr Liddell spoke to Mick, Jim crossed the courtyard and entered the house through the double doors. His father had not turned on the lights, and the chairs and sofa, rugs and fireplace were shadowy. Ahead was a wall made entirely of wood, with a long, low bookcase across it, which Jim had heard Mrs Griswold call a 'feature wall'. While the voices of Mick and his father faded behind him, and Paulie's music softened to the edge of silence, Jim touched the feature wall with his fingertips, and found himself at his mother's door.

• • •

Not so long ago, the room had belonged to both his parents, but then his mother had fallen sick, and his father had moved to the spare room across the hall, which had only a single bed, wardrobe, dressing table and ladder-backed chair in it.

Since his mother had returned from the hospital yesterday morning, with the illness that had made her sick for months finally cured, her door had been shut. Jim had gone in only twice, with his father, and both times she had been asleep.

At his first visit to the hospital Jim had been angry to find a cosy room containing a stack of history books and a little TV set. Without his mother, home had become a mere heap of bricks, wood and glass, hardly even a shelter. A place that might have been any place. She seemed to have taken the true home with her, to the hospital.

His mother's door was painted a mysterious green-blue. He touched it with his fingertips, the way he had the feature wall. Ages ago he had found a stone at the Tacker Bay Estuary exactly the colour of this door. He had picked it up and now kept it in his desk drawer.

Jim's father had warned him not to enter his mother's room when the door was closed.

'She's sleeping. She needs a lot of sleep, to recover from her operation.'

Jim moved his fingers to the handle.

He had to see her. If she was asleep, he would simply tiptoe out again, and no harm would have been done. If she was awake he would tell her about Mudlark.

He turned the handle, and pushed the door a fraction into the afternoon glow of sunlight against blinds and curtains.

He widened the gap, and chilly air from the water-cooler caught him in the face.

A white wall came into view, then a table on wheels shaped like a U sideways, that fitted both underneath and over the bed, and was now crowded with bottles of medicine and pills, a roll of white cottonwool, scissors, and a white bowl that looked to be empty. Next came the bed, at first seeming made-up and unused, until his mother came into view.

Her short dark hair was parted to one side, her hands were folded over her chest. Her eyes were closed. But instead of warning Jim, this reassured him. He hadn't woken her by opening the door. So now he closed it soundlessly and crept towards her, wishing he'd thought to take off his shoes.

Beside the table next to her was an oxygen cylinder, which was black with the paint chipped off in a few places, showing the grey metal underneath, with a brass valve and nozzle at its top. The mask, which fitted closely over nose and mouth, was on the table, connected to the valve by a plastic tube. Both mask and tube were the same mysterious green-blue as her door, perhaps a fraction brighter.

The room darkened as the sun finally set over the Brownscombes' house across the road.

Taking care not to bump into anything in the increasing gloom, Jim was leaving when his mother spoke:

'Jim?'

'Oh —'

'No, no,' she hurried on, pushing with her elbows to move herself higher on the bed. 'I must have dozed off. I'm feeling much better. No pain at all. If the doctor doesn't let me out of bed soon, I'm going to rebel. What time is it?'

'Um …'

'After school, anyway?'

'Yes.'

'Come and sit down.' She patted the mattress and tucked a strand of hair behind an ear. 'Have they told you that you mustn't come in here?'

Jim nodded. And seeing his mother's face up close, he wanted to laugh, and hug her, because she did look better. Gone were the shadows over her eyes, and the extreme thinness that had allowed him to see the outline of her teeth through the skin.

She held his hand.

'I'll be up soon. What shall we do then, together?'

Now Jim did laugh, though softly, so that no-one outside would hear and come to interrupt.

'It's holidays soon,' she went on, 'and do you know what I've always wanted to do, and what I promised myself in hospital that I would do when I got better, with you?'

'No. What?'

'Go down to the end of the Creek in Clyde Pharr's canoe. He's offered to lend it to us often enough, hasn't he? But what have you been doing today, Jim? Tell me.'

'I have Mudlark, the class bird, home for the weekend. Do you want me to go and get him now, to show you?'

'No, no. I'll be able to get up by myself very soon, and I don't want Dad getting angry. It's not his fault, it's what the doctors told him. All nonsense, of course, this bed-rest, but we need to keep your visits a secret. Will you come again tomorrow? When Dad is out?'

'Yes, I will.'

'Where is he now?'

'Out the back, talking to Mick Ryan.'

'You'd better go then. Say hello to Mudlark for me.'

'I will. Goodbye.'

4

It was Mr Liddell who ordered the pizza, and delivered pieces on clean plates, still wet underneath from having just been washed, to Jim and Paulie in their rooms. Then he ate a single slice alone in front of the TV, with work from the office on a coffee-table beside him and feet up on a chair from the dining room.

No-one had turned on the living-room lights, so Mr Liddell sat and worked, and ate his piece of pizza, and drank a bottle of Mick Ryan's beer, in the light from the flickering TV screen.

Jim placed his Journal between Mudlark and the plate and wrote a few lines in continuation of a story about Behemoth in the golf-course, and how two boys followed the monster to its lair, and there watched in horror as it crunched up old bones in its powerful jaws.

Then he closed the book, and took a deep breath. Yes, one day he really would go into the golf-course, and find Behemoth.

He dropped the Journal into his bag, and went to his desk.

'Well, Mudlark. Time for you to talk.'

The bird glanced at him, then faced the other way.

Jim lowered his voice. 'It's okay. No-one else can hear.'

Mudlark stayed facing away, silent.

'Oh, I remember,' Jim went on. 'You spoke to Sam when it was dark, in the middle of the night. All right then, I'll read for a while, then when it's time to go to sleep I'll turn off the light, and we can have a talk. Okay?'

• • •

So Jim read, while faint and sadly beautiful music came from Paulie's room, joined with the distant voices of the TV.

'All right now,' he announced firmly, putting out the light and getting beneath the covers.

'Guess what, Mudlark? I'm not going to sleep until you talk.'

Silence.

'Well, come on. Please. What do you have to lose? Paulie can't hear anything but his music, and my father's watching TV. My mother's right over the other side of the house, with her door closed.'

Silence.

'You spoke for Sam, didn't you?'

And here, for the first time, Jim doubted. Had Sam been telling the truth?

Of course he had.

'Mudlark?'

Silence.

And then relief came over him, as he thought out loud:

'But why *should* you talk, if you don't feel like it?

You hardly know me, after all. Or you might not be in the mood for it. As simple as that. You aren't a toy to be turned on or off whenever I want. So don't worry, Mudlark. You don't have to talk if you don't want to. Just being in my room is enough. Yes it is. But do you mind if I talk? Just whistle if you want to go to sleep. Did I tell you that my mother's getting up tomorrow, or the day after? In my desk drawer, underneath you, at the back, is a stone that's exactly the colour of her door.'

The bird listened in silence as Jim's words became less and less connected to one another, became mumbles, and were replaced by deep breathing.

Moonlight fell across the map of the world, then in a line along Mudlark's beak as the bird raised his head to gaze at the bright sickle shape floating in darkness.

Paulie stopped playing, had a shower, and read through a few pages of a music score before turning off his light.

Mr Liddell dozed at the TV, head tipped back and mouth open, snoring softly, until a particularly loud commercial shook him awake, and he blinked without recognition at the screen and at the papers scattered on the coffee-table. He stood up, stretched, crept across the room, gently eased open the door to his wife's room, and whispered, 'Are you awake?' Then he waited for a while, listening to her breathing, before closing the door soundlessly again.

Jim opened his eyes. Sunlight was pouring through the window, and Mudlark was singing at the top of his voice.

But Jim's face was damp, and as he pushed back the covers his hands were trembling. He rushed for his Journal, and wrote:

A monster in the dark? No, more a nightmare. You know it's there, but you don't know where to run. You could never run fast enough, anyway.

PART TWO

5

Miles to the south of Tacker Bay, storm clouds were gathering. But except on weather reports, heard over breakfast, or in cars on the way to shops or to cricket or netball matches, there was no sign of them, this Saturday morning, in Tacker Bay itself.

Jim got himself cornflakes, and this time discovered two plastic bottles of milk in the refrigerator. And next to the sink was a loaf of bread. His father had been shopping, then, although he seemed to be nowhere around now. The door to the spare room stood open. Sheets and blankets were in a heap at the foot of the bed. Jim put his ear to his mother's door and heard a faint voice that might have been his father, or perhaps it was Dr Cunningham.

Making for his bedroom and Mudlark, he nearly dropped the bowl of cornflakes when he saw Sam in the courtyard with his head on fire — but it was only sunlight caught in his orange hair.

Sam took a step back before his friend's astonished gaze.

'I said I'd come over this morning to see Mudlark. You're still in your school uniform. You slept in your clothes?'

'No.' Jim took a deep breath. It had shocked him, that was all, seeing Sam there like something out of the terrible, unremembered dream that he had had last night. 'No, these aren't my school clothes. They're a disguise.'

'What?'

'Do you want something to eat?'

'No thanks. How's Mudlark?'

'Come and see.'

The bird glanced from face to face, then flew to the topmost perch to resume staring out the window.

Sam spoke thoughtfully:

'You know, he looks different to how he does in the classroom. Bigger.'

While Jim changed hastily into a T-shirt and jeans, Sam pointed and said, 'Look, there's hardly any water left. In fact, there isn't any. Can you see, Jim?'

Yes, fastened to the cage by twists of wire, the bowl contained no water at all.

'Also,' Sam mentioned in his slow way that could be annoying when it was something you didn't want to hear, 'the sunlight's shining directly in. He might be dying of thirst, or of heatstroke. You shouldn't keep him in the sunlight.'

'Oh yes, he really looks like he's dying,' Jim mocked.

But he ran straight to the kitchen, doing up his jeans, and returned with a plastic measuring jug half-full of water, one of the many kitchen utensils not used by anyone since his mother had entered the hospital.

He placed this against the cage. The spout was just too wide to fit between the bars.

'You have to —' began Sam.

'I know. Take the bowl out.'

'Yes.'

Jim started to raise the door.

'Wait.' Sam jumped up and closed the bedroom door. 'He might get out.' He went to the window, open at the top, and pushed it shut.

'Why don't we let him out, to fly around the room a bit?' Jim.

'How would we get him back in?'

'Just pick him up. He's tame. He isn't frightened of us.'

'We might hurt him.'

Yet Sam's protest was weak enough to make it plain that he was attracted by the idea.

'And I can clean his cage then, too, and give him a new newspaper to read.'

'What if someone opens the door?'

'They won't. My mother's in bed, and can't get up until Monday. My father's out, and Paulie never comes in here unless I ask him to.'

Sam was silent. And for these moments it was as if

the whole of Tacker Bay was silent too. And this was only broken when slow, sleepy, soft trumpet music started up in Paulie's near-soundproofed room.

'Your brother certainly can play,' murmured Sam.

Jim checked that his own door was closed, glanced again at the window, and raised the door to Mudlark's cage.

The bird turned his intelligent, dark eyes from Jim to Sam, and back to Jim. He hopped to the bottom perch, and tilted his head at the doorway. And then in one clean hop, helped along by a flutter of wings, he flew out of the cage and across the room, to perch high on the wardrobe door.

'See him fly!' Jim admired.

Glancing now and then at Mudlark, Sam had already taken out the water bowl and was carefully filling it from the jug.

Mudlark flew to the window, as Sam fastened the bowl back inside.

'Did he talk to you?' he asked.

'No.' Without looking at his friend, he added: 'Did he really talk to you?'

Sam didn't answer, straight away.

From the curtain rod, Mudlark gazed calmly down at the boys.

'I think he did,' Sam finally replied. 'But it's possible that I dreamt it. How are we going to get him down?'

Dreamt it. The words had such a dull sound. They faded quickly away.

Jim sighed.

Mudlark looked tiny, up there. Perhaps he was just an ordinary bird, and couldn't talk at all.

The white streaks on his wings shone in the shadows. He opened one and stretched it right out, then did the same with the other. Sitting calmly up there, he seemed to be waiting for something.

'Should we —?' began Sam.

At that instant, the top part of Jim's window slipped down, six inches.

Before the boys could get over their astonishment, before they could even start to rush over and push the window back up, Mudlark hopped to the gap.

He perched on the window, glanced at the backyard with its trees and sky, and whole universe just beyond. Nothing lay between him and it, no bars or glass, nothing at all. He turned back to the boys, raised one wing, lowered it again, faced the yard, and was gone.

'Oh God,' groaned Jim.

Both boys simply gazed at the gap in the window, as though hoping that what they had seen would turn out to be an illusion — that the window had never really opened, that Mudlark would still be on top of the curtain rail, about to be captured.

They broke the spell at the same moment. Jim shouted, 'Quick!' as they rushed into the backyard, fresh morning air in their faces, Jim's bare feet in the moist grass.

The sky was pure blue and empty. No bird in the branches of the pepper tree, nor in the frangipani that grew in Mrs Hogan's garden and overhung the Liddells'. No Mudlark on the guttering, gazing down at them. They advanced, peering into the pepper tree, then into the high branches of the paperbark.

'Gone,' Sam couldn't help whispering.

Jim ran to the opposite side, where new people had just moved in, a man and woman and a baby, but saw no bird in the branches of their trees.

'I did shut the window,' Sam muttered. 'I pushed it right up. It went 'clunk'.'

'I know. The cord at the side gets caught. It hasn't happened in ages. In years. I'd forgotten about it. It was my fault.'

As the boys stood in the birdless garden, Paulie was playing what sounded like a lament for the disappearance of all precious things, of what you would most like to keep and never lose. Their bird, their whole class's bird, Mr Bennet's beloved pet, had gone.

All year, week after week, every Friday, boys had taken Mudlark home, and this had never happened. Never.

Back in his bedroom, the empty cage, blue bowl full of water, tray at the bottom half pulled-out ready for fresh sheets of newspaper, made Jim's mind go blank from shock.

'In an instant,' he mumbled. 'Just one moment,

and everything is changed. Your whole life can change in one moment, and you can never have it back the way it was.'

He would have cried if suddenly Mudlark's disappearance hadn't struck him as not only terribly unfair, but also as a sort of lie.

He ran back into the garden and rushed all around, peering into every tree and along every gutter.

Turning at the end of this search he bumped into Sam, and before he knew what he was doing he had pushed him away with both hands. And when his friend stumbled, and fell onto the grass, Jim advanced as though to hit him, but instead found himself shouting:

'Stay away from me! It wasn't your fault, I know, but now Mudlark's gone, and everything's different. I'm going to look for him by myself. And ... and ...'

And now he really didn't know what he was saying. A part of his mind reeled in surprise to hear:

'And if I haven't found him by tonight, do you know what I'm going to do? I'm going into the golf-course, I'm going there by myself when it's dark and no-one else is around, and I'm going to find Behemoth!'

Although used to hearing bizarre things from Jim, Sam had expected nothing like this. He nodded assent, brushed dew and grass from his pants, and took another step back. He was about to say something not at all angry, but sympathetic, when Jim — sensing this — interrupted.

'Go, then! And maybe I'll see you tonight, either with Mudlark or on my way to the golf-course to capture Behemoth.'

He raised one arm to further solemnify this vow, and his face had never been paler, nor his eyes darker.

Jim stood in his room, arms folded, staring at the six-inch gap in his window, and waiting until he could be certain that Sam had gone. Then he put on a pair of canvas shoes, tying the laces carefully in long bows, which he knotted and re-knotted. He pushed the window right up, then stood back to see what happened.

It stayed up.

Only that one time had it slipped down. With Mudlark perched on the curtain rail, just above. Perhaps the bird had sensed what was about to happen. Hadn't he stretched his wings, waiting for the window to slip?

To get the window down, Jim had to tug at it.

He would leave it open, the cage door too, in case Mudlark came home.

He closed the door to his room though, so that his father or Paulie wouldn't see the empty cage.

Next to the bathroom door was a linen cupboard that contained sheets and blankets folded and stacked into tidy columns. Since Jim's mother had got sick, no-one had folded away a single sheet. When the dirty-clothes basket filled up, Mr Liddell would add to it all the sheets and pillowcases in the house and take it to the Tacker Bay laundrette before work, and that evening would place everything cleaned and dried on the dining table for Jim and Paulie to sort through.

Running the backs of his fingers against the folded sheets, Jim momentarily longed to rush into his mother's room to tell her what had happened. Certainly, no doubt at all, she would know what he should do. As carefully as her hands had folded these sheets, weeks and weeks ago, her words would arrange and order his fears. But he couldn't. Either his father or Dr Cunningham was with her, or she was asleep.

Mr Bennet had found Mudlark by the Creek, wounded by other birds for trespassing on their territory.

Jim had to find him, and quickly.

A blanket would be too heavy. He had often helped his mother make beds. Sheets would billow, and have to be patted down. He needed something lighter than a blanket, yet heavier than a sheet, as a net for Mudlark.

He ran his knuckles over folded sheets, white and pale shades of blue, then, stooping lower, over green blankets that were only ever taken out in winter, until he came to the perfect thing at the bottom.

Net-like, blue cloth so broadly woven that you could see through it — the exact blanket, he had been told, that had kept him warm as a baby.

Pushing back the stack above to keep it from toppling, he pulled it out.

Half the size of a normal blanket, which was just right too. He unfolded and swung it like a bullfighter's cape, and because of the holes in the weave — each about the size of the fingernail on his little finger — it went cleanly through the air: no billowing.

Perfect for catching Mudlark.

Cheered by this discovery, and also somehow by the feel of the infinitely soft stuff from which the blanket was made, he half-rolled, half-folded it, ran to his room, tipped out everything from his backpack, and stuffed in the blanket. Then he pulled his Journal and a pen from the desk drawer and wrote quickly:

Until now he had believed that adventures existed only in books and films and that real life was the dullest thing ever invented.

He paused, and added:

Behemoth in his forest. Yes, that was what truly frightened him.

He added the Journal and pen to the outer pocket of the pack and, thumbs around straps, yanking it higher on his back, ran into the backyard.

6

After the gentle shadows of the linen cupboard, the sunlight in the yard made him halt, and blink. Eyes narrowed, shading them with a hand, he advanced to the old pepper tree. Its trunk was ancient and knotted, its branches so hard they might have been made of metal, yet the delicate leaves trembled in the lightest breeze.

He climbed to the first fork and was peering into labyrinths of branches and twigs and green light, when a darker, more pointed kind of movement caught his attention.

He crawled along a branch until the source of this came into view, caught in a square of bright blue.

Mudlark.

Certainly Mudlark, from the way he poked his beak beneath a wing, feathers fanned out, then gazed calmly at Jim with his own utterly Mudlarkian thoughtfulness.

'A game,' the look seemed to say. 'This is a game that will end soon, with you capturing me. In the meantime, let's have some fun.'

Jim found himself giving a laugh in reply, as the blue square suddenly became empty.

Craning, he glimpsed Mudlark in flight and — as he jumped from the tree — managed to note that the bird had alighted on the topmost branch of the frangipani tree in Mrs Hogan's backyard.

Jim took out the blanket. Must be careful, he told himself, when Mudlark is in it, to be gentle, as gentle as possible, reaching in and holding the bird.

'Their hollow bones,' Mr Bennet had told the class, 'make birds not only light enough to fly, but also extremely delicate. Those who soar the highest,' he had added, 'such as Mudlark here, are the most delicate of all.'

Jim pulled himself onto the fence's crossbar, and from there to the corrugated iron roof of the gardening shed that went within a metre of the frangipani tree's topmost branch. The perfect launching pad for the blanket.

Among the yellow-white flowers, Mudlark turned his head in sharp, jerky movements, looking in every direction.

A dark shape passed across the back windows of Mrs Hogan's house.

Jim stayed still, telling himself that there was nothing to be frightened of. A shadow, he had seen a shadow, that was all.

Meanwhile, the grass of Mrs Hogan's lawn had sunk into a green so deep that it was almost purple. The frangipani petals shone white, the yellow at their centres glowing like drops of molten gold.

Even Mudlark looked frightened at this sudden change in the day. He fluffed up his feathers and tucked down his head.

Unfolding the blanket, Jim glanced at the sky. A cloud had covered the sun. That was all.

Yet he couldn't help linking this sudden darkness to the shadowy movement at the back windows of Mrs Hogan's house.

Witches are merely characters in stories, he warned himself.

They do not exist.

The corrugations in the iron roof made little crunching sounds as his shoes pressed them down.

Mudlark was hardly two metres away, now a metre and a half. Easy throwing distance for the blanket.

At such important moments, time can move slowly.

Jim took another crunching step, and had begun to cast the blanket the way he had seen fishermen cast nets in films, when Mudlark gave a little hop, opened his wings, and at that moment Jim's foot sank into the roof.

This made a really huge, crunching sound, and caused him to topple forwards.

The blanket netted nothing but frangipani blossoms, and as Jim fell these flowers brushed his face, their petals noticeably cold. Mostly the branches bent, but one or two snapped as he tumbled through them to find himself among leaves and dirt on the ground.

Now the blanket was over his head, and on the thumb of his right hand was a single, brilliantly white drop of frangipani sap.

Carefully lifting the blanket — unsure whether he might not have caught Mudlark anyway — he knelt, and just as it registered that he had not broken any bones, or cut himself, he heard Mrs Hogan's back door open.

What scared him, what caused him to panic through a tangle of baby-blanket and flowers, wasn't this sound, but the silence that followed.

He got to his feet, to find Mrs Hogan's face an inch from his own.

'You had better come into the house,' was all she said.

Her fingers went around his arm, cool and strong.

His legs felt as if his solid, human bones had become hollow, like a bird's. Hanging by one strap, his backpack started to fall off. He pulled it back up. With his other hand he clutched the blanket to his chest.

Obviously he was the victim of an enchantment. Useless to struggle.

They climbed the steps. A tap dripped through miles of silence into a metal sink. The kitchen was dark. Jim halted by the door. Mrs Hogan let go of his arm.

'Come inside, Jim.'

Caught by the spell, he couldn't help obeying. The floor was white linoleum, with a pattern of grey swirls. He had never been here before.

Mrs Hogan opened a cupboard and brought out a hand-towel.

'So, are you all right, Jim?'

He said nothing.

She ran water onto a corner of the towel, then dabbed it to his forehead.

'Only dirt. Skin not broken. Does anything hurt?'

'No,' he managed to answer, voice coming out as a croak.

Now that she has me at her mercy, he was thinking, what will she do? He pictured his mother's and father's sorrow at his disappearance, and tears nearly came to his eyes.

He imagined a policeman informing them, 'No news, none whatsoever. Seems to have vanished without a trace.'

'Are you all right, Jim?' Mrs Hogan persisted. 'Are you sure you didn't hit your head? You look terribly pale. But then you always look pale, don't you?'

In the silence that followed, as she examined or pretended to examine him for cuts and bruises, he was able to think clearly.

Real terror was so different from how he had imagined it. Although his mind was racing, his legs felt paralysed. The only reason he didn't beg for mercy was that he didn't have enough air in his lungs, and might suffocate if he spoke.

'That roof.' Mrs Hogan nodded towards her backyard. 'I'm glad you knocked the corner of it off, because it's a good excuse for me to get the shed pulled down and have something built, something I've always wanted. Do you know what that is, Jim? A glasshouse. Yes, one made entirely of glass, and inside it I plan to grow orchids. Glass lets sunlight in, but won't allow much heat out. Orchids. Ever seen one? Strange flowers. Thousands of types. A friend of mine used to grow them. Anyhow, why don't you go into the living room and sit down, and I'll bring you a piece of cake and a cup of tea. Have you had lunch, Jim?'

He shook his head. Was it that late?

'I didn't think so. I'll bring you a sandwich. Go and sit down. There are plenty of books. Feel free to read one.'

He found himself entering the next room.

A ceiling fan stirred the leaves of potplants on a window-ledge. Waist-high bookshelves went across two walls.

Jim took off his backpack and sat down.

Mrs Hogan opened and closed the refrigerator.

Finally, Jim took a deep breath.

So, she had decided against using her powers to make him disappear, or to change him into something. She had been about to do it, but had changed her mind.

Why? Something to do with the shed ... the glasshouse ... orchids? Her memory of the friend who had liked orchids, perhaps.

As he pushed the blue blanket into the backpack, he wondered briefly why he had it with him. He remembered with a feeling of relief.

So, it looked like Mudlark was going to stay nearby. He would catch him this morning, definitely.

The bookshelf nearest him contained a mixture of paperbacks and hardbacks, with one volume an inch or two taller than the others. This one's spine was bare leather, no writing on it. What else could it be, except a book of spells?

Jim glanced at the doorway, and quickly took it out. No letters on the front either. He opened the cover.

Holy Bible, said the title page. The leather cover merely surrounded a smaller, black, ordinary one.

He was holding apart the other books on the shelf, and pushing the Bible back in, when a tiny piece of paper slipped out. He hurriedly picked it up.

It was an ancient, yellowed newspaper cutting. One side contained rows of tiny numbers, but on the other was a news item.

DEATH OF A MOTORCYCLIST

Shortly after three o'clock yesterday afternoon, at the intersection of Liverpool Street and Old South Head Road, Tacker Bay, a young man was killed when his motorcycle collided with a motor vehicle. A pillion passenger, the fiancée of the deceased, was taken to hospital, where she remains in a satisfactory condition.

Jim looked up to see Mrs Hogan across the table, holding a tray that supported a pot of tea, cups and saucers, and a plate of sandwiches cut into triangles.

'Yes,' she murmured, as though continuing a conversation begun in the kitchen, 'that fiancée, that girl, was me. And I still remember that day, at the intersection of Liverpool Street and Old South Head Road, as clearly as I do seeing you fall through a cloud of frangipani blossoms just now.'

She laid the tray on the table and began to take off the things. Jim carefully inserted the scrap of paper back inside the Bible.

'It was a sunny day like this morning, before those clouds came along, and Geoff and I were completely, entirely happy. Better than that — we were happy, and knew it. I had my arms around his waist and there we were, riding up Liverpool Street, and a second later a car driven by an old man took the turn a fraction too wide, and … well, you've read the article. Please, have a sandwich.'

Jim took a triangle. The bread was soft, fresh. Inside was ham, lettuce and tomato.

Mrs Hogan went on.

'You've probably already guessed, Jim. I'll bet you have.'

'The orchids,' he found himself saying. 'Your friend …'

'Geoff.'

'Yes, he was the one who had the glasshouse and the orchids.'

Mrs Hogan's whole face was covered in wrinkles. Beneath her chin, folds of skin hung down and waggled back and forth as she spoke.

Yet as Jim watched her, sitting upright so as to see her eyes through the top rather than the bottom of her glasses, he succeeded for a moment in picturing her as she had been over fifty years ago. A girl with dark eyes, hair pulled back and caught up in a ponytail bound around with a plain old rubberband.

He gave a start. Sandra Brownscombe. He had been seeing young Mrs Hogan as Sandra Brownscombe.

'Yes, Jim,' Mrs Hogan was saying. 'He was a gardener, with a passion for orchids. It wasn't long afterwards that I met Eloise, my talking cat. Perhaps I went crazy for a while, or perhaps she really did talk. And you, Jim, will you do me a favour?'

'Yes, Mrs Hogan.'

'Call me Sonya. Will you do that?'

'Yes … Sonya.'

'Apart from your mother and father, and your brother Paulie, you don't have many relatives, do you?'

'No. My father has a brother who lives in America. I only met him once, when I was little.'

'Well, I would like to think, Jim, that if you are ever in trouble, or need someone to talk to, about anything at all, or a bit of help, you will come to me. I'm not really a witch, although of course I would very much like to be one, if such creatures existed. Now I suppose I had better let you go. Look, the sun has come out again. What a strange day this is.'

At one side of the windowsill, the leaves were full of light.

Jim found himself on the back step.

'And Jim …' The old woman held out her arms in a sweeping gesture. 'My backyard is yours. House too, of course. Feel free to explore as much as you wish. Just think of me as a kind of relation living next door.'

• • •

A path made of bricks branched to the shed and garbage bin on the right — with two or three sparkles of broken glass still here and there — and directly ahead disappeared into a garden made of such deep shadow that the rare patches of sunlight looked frail and out of place.

Jim wondered what Mrs Hogan — Sonya — was doing now. Leaving the house perhaps, going for a walk by the golf-course, down to the Tacker Bay shops — or even further, to the Creek or the Bay.

Alone. Was she always alone? He had never seen her with anyone else.

At the corner of the shed the guttering had fallen down, spilling a heap of ancient, brown frangipani leaves.

Jim advanced down the shadowed path, looking confidently into the branches of the eucalyptus trees until he glimpsed an intense glimmer of black and white high, high up.

He tried to run, but ivy tugged at his feet, so he took short strides, bringing each knee up high as though wading through water, until he came to the fence and what appeared to be the ruins of a barbecue. From here he couldn't see Mudlark, so he stepped back, stumbling in the ivy. As he reached for a tree-trunk to support himself, he saw the bird race across blueness, along the lit-up edge of a cloud, and finally out of sight behind the bushes in the garden next to Mrs Hogan's.

Jim climbed from barbecue to fencetop and jumped down on the other side, between bushes, onto bare earth.

7

Beyond lawns or shrubs, out of reach of paths and washing lines, these far ends of backyards are secret, forgotten places, and to Jim it seemed only right that he and Mudlark should find themselves here.

Apart from the faintest possible background hum, which might have been traffic on Old South Head Road or a breeze in the treetops, the silence was complete. When it was broken by a whole flurry of noises, Jim found himself reacting even before he had identified the source.

He ran, grabbed a splintery fencetop with both hands, jumped, and got one leg up, then the other. Grazing the underside of one arm, he twisted around and fell to the grass on the other side.

The dog collided with the planks behind him, then barked with amazing loudness, jaws inches from where Jim was getting to his feet.

'Rollo! Rollo! What are you doing? What have you got there?' came a woman's voice as Jim ran, bent double.

Rollo stayed right beside him, inches away on the other side of the palings, until Jim came to next-door's fence. He hurried a metre or two down this before climbing it, so that Rollo's owner wouldn't see him.

He had never seen this next backyard before, not even from high in his own pepper tree. It was entirely grass. No cover at all between him and the house. Worse, the back door was open.

So, as Rollo's barking stopped — though the noise seemed to have permanently killed the gentle hum of traffic — Jim ran, doubled over, and climbed the next fence.

Each backyard was a separate universe. For an instant Jim felt sad at the thought that even in a whole, long lifetime, no-one could explore all the backyards in the world.

Wooden fruit-boxes were stacked at the bottom of this next yard, and a brick building — a garage, he guessed — hid him from the back of the house. A concrete path led through spongy, tough grass, to an iron clothes hoist on which hung three white T-shirts, Y-front underpants, and a pair of dark blue shorts.

Jim caught his breath, and examined the graze on his arm. Although it stung fiercely, it wasn't bleeding. He pulled away a sliver of skin so thin that it was nearly transparent, rolled it into a ball, and flicked it towards the clothes hoist.

Mudlark was nearby, he was certain of it. He would be travelling in short bursts, because after more than a year in a cage his wings would not be accustomed to flying.

Jim again took out the blanket, and advanced into this new backyard-world.

The door at the back of the house was closed and yet now, for the first time since his ears had stopped ringing from Rollo's barking, he heard music.

Was it Paulie, from several yards away? No. He held his breath. A man was singing, too softly or too far away for Jim to make out the words.

Then a familiar movement caught his eyes, and he turned, and smiled.

Mudlark had alighted on the far side of the clothes hoist, between two white T-shirts.

Advancing one slow step at a time, Jim wondered if he would even need the blue blanket. Surely Mudlark would allow him to reach out and hold him. And if the bird ever wanted to get out of the cage again, and explore this world of backyards, why, Jim would be happy to let him.

A breeze ruffled the bird's feathers and Jim's hair, and made the T-shirts lean away and fall back, as boy and bird came closer, closer.

Then Jim was standing beside Mudlark, within easy reaching distance. He extended his arm, but Mudlark shook his head, gave the little hop that Jim knew all too well by now, and flew up and across in the direction of the garage.

The boy shook his head as though waking from a trance.

'That's it!' he muttered.

Mudlark could explore backyards all he wanted, but later. This was enough for today.

Holding tightly on to the blanket, keeping an eye on the back windows of the apparently deserted house, he ran towards the garage and sped up around the corner, expecting to see Mudlark on the fence. Instead he heard louder singing, and before he could slow down, felt a hard edge against his chest and saw a man's face looking so astonished that at first he didn't recognise it.

The man staggered back, into a cave full of golden light.

Jim had time to notice that Mudlark wasn't on the fence, was nowhere about.

'Wait! Yah! Hey!' the man shouted.

A wooden box fell from his hands. He bumped into a row of glass vats. One toppled, and smashed. Fine white froth poured over the garage floor.

Now a hand gripped Jim's shoulder. A face shot up close, swollen with anger, more threatening than anything Jim had ever seen. Already shadowy, the air grew cold. An awful taste came into Jim's mouth. This wasn't a man, it was pure anger, anger in the form of a person and capable of anything.

This lasted only a moment, yet it struck Jim as a moment powerful enough to change a person's life.

Then the face retreated and the emotion drew back, like the wash from a gigantic wave down a beach, and a familiar voice said, 'Ah there!'

Glancing at the froth over the concrete floor, wet broken glass amid the planks of a broken fruit-box, he added, 'To what do I owe the pleasure of this most unexpected visit?'

Mick Ryan folded his bare, muscly arms. The hairs on his chest were mostly grey. The skin was stretched tight across his face into a grin more like a mask than any real expression.

'I'm so sorry.' Without realising it, Jim had moved away. 'I was after my bird.'

Mick stepped aside to contemplate the damage.

'A few bottles. One vat. One crate.'

He sighed. Now his smile shone out with a warmth as golden as the glimmers of light within the beer bottles around him.

'Nothing,' he concluded. 'Absolutely nothing.'

'I'll pay for it,' Jim offered feebly, conscious that he had no money.

'Wouldn't think of it.' Mick rubbed his bare arms. 'Getting kind of chilly, isn't it?'

He stepped past Jim, jogged to the clothes hoist, unpegged a T-shirt, and when he had pulled it on, gestured towards the back of the house.

'Want something to eat?'

'No ... thank you. I need to find my bird.'

'And what bird might that be?'

Before Jim could answer, he gestured at the darkening sky. 'Will you look at that? Lovely day, going to ruin. Sorry ... you were saying? What kind of bird did you lose?'

Both Jim and Mick found themselves gazing around, or pretending to do so.

'Mudlark, a mudlark.'

'Ah, like a little magpie. Build their nests out of mud, down by the Creek?'

Jim nodded. 'Only this one doesn't come from around here. My teacher found him being pecked at by other birds, and put him in a cage for his own good. I got to take him home for the weekend, but he got out.'

'Got out,' Mick repeated thoughtfully. 'And now he might prefer being attacked to being in a cage?'

'Yes, he might.'

'And you're out to catch him? You're the police, in pursuit of a jailbird?'

'Or …'

'Or a boy in search of a lost bird. Of course. Well, if I see a tame mudlark, I'll grab him for you. That's a promise. Have you thought of looking down by the Creek?'

'Yes, but he doesn't seem to want to fly very far right now.'

'Well, he'll probably make his way down there sooner or later. All that mud. I bet he can smell it. Plus, there's the companionship of his fellow creatures. However dangerous that might be, he'll seek it out. They always do. We always do. And there's supposed to be a cave down there. Heard about it? Never seen it myself, though old Clyde Pharr swears it exists. A cave where mudlarks go when they're hurt, badly hurt, or …' Mick trailed off, pushing his hands into his pockets.

'But I'm wasting your time,' he briskly resumed. 'If I can't tempt you to come inside for a snack, I'd better let you get on with your search.'

As Jim turned to go, a hand brushed his arm.

'And I'm sorry' — Mick spoke softly — 'I lost my temper. Listen, come and visit me, soon. If you want to earn some pocket-money, you could help me with my beer. There's always rinsing and bottling to do, and I pay good wages. Or if you just want a chat, come anyway.'

Jim nodded beneath the weight of this kindness, and ran towards the street, his street, Faraday Avenue.

8

His room was dark. Was the day nearly over? Yet surely it had just begun. He didn't wear a watch, because he usually forgot to put it on when he woke up or after a shower, and then would spend ages searching for it.

Mudlark's empty cage was even darker than the rest of the room. The water in the little blue bowl looked icy. Difficult to believe that this was the very cage that had stood all year beside Mr Bennet's desk.

Jim put his head in his hands, then sat upright quickly, frightened. Without warning, he had felt like crying.

It was hopeless.

Hopeless, hopeless, hopeless.

Mick Ryan was right. Mudlark would make for the Creek. And down there were hundreds of mudlarks — young and old, small and full-grown — and even if they didn't peck Mudlark to death, how would he, Jim, ever tell his Mudlark from all the other birds?

Mudlark was gone forever.

Jim was hungry, yet did not wish to eat. The hollowness in his stomach felt like something that would never go away. Standing by the linen cupboard, he remembered Mick Ryan's anger, and shivered. The house was silent. He listened for the trumpet, and made out a faint tune, fast and cheerful, that seemed to mock his unhappiness.

He wandered from bathroom to kitchen, putting off doing what he knew that he shouldn't do.

And at last he found himself before his mother's

room, fingers against the blue-green paint. He stepped away, and opened the front door. His father's car wasn't in the driveway. He turned the handle of his mother's door, easing it open.

Into view came the trolley-table full of pills and medicines, the empty half of the bed, and finally his mother. She was not only awake but pushing herself up on one elbow and twisting stiffly around to reach the bedside light.

'Thank heavens you came, Jim.' And all at once the cold darkness not merely of this room, but of the whole house, was dispelled. With its warm light, the bedside lamp confirmed this.

'Thank heavens. I was being lazy, just lying here. It's the pills that do it. Meant to take away pain, but all they do is make me feel sleepy. And it's high time for me to have some oxygen.'

She turned the little black wheel at the cylinder's valve, and picked up the greeny-blue mask. The hiss of the gas was hardly a sound, more a gentle underlining of the room's silence. Mask lightly over mouth and nose, she took one, two, three deep breaths. Then she laid it on her lap and patted the bed.

'Come and sit down. What's wrong?'

He sat, and told her the story of Mudlark's escape.

'I've spent all day looking for him. I'll never find him now. I know it.' Tears came to his eyes. 'I feel terrible. I'm frightened of people. I feel all alone sometimes. All alone.'

As Jim spoke, Mrs Liddell again raised the mask to her face.

Except for the part about Mudlark, Jim had not planned to say any of this. Likewise without thinking, he added:

'I don't fit in. I'm not like anyone else. I can't help imagining things, all the time. I tell lies, too. Yesterday morning I told Mr Harding, the new deputy-headmaster, that you and Dad were dead.'

He covered his face with his hands.

From behind the blinded and curtained window came the rumble of thunder.

Mrs Liddell placed the mask back on the table, sat upright, put her arms around her younger son, and pulled him closer. In the lamp's yellow light, they might have been twins. Same straight nose, pale skin, dark eyes.

'Jim, Jim, Jim …'

His crying died away, and he took his hands from his face and started to wipe his nose with the back of one, and his eyes with the other, when he felt soft stuff — tissues — against his fingers.

'Here, use those.'

Head bowed, paying careful attention, she began to turn off the oxygen cylinder's valve.

'Aren't you supposed to —?' he started to protest.

'No, no, that's enough for now. There'll be all the time in the world for deep breathing when I get up. Give me your hand, Jim.'

He transferred the tissues to his left and, still wiping his nose, gave her his right.

'Jim, what you said —'

'Oh, I didn't mean —'

'No, please. Let me finish.'

She was silent for a moment, thinking.

'Jim, you're right. You're perfectly right. You are different from others. You *do* imagine. You do dream, more than anyone I've ever known. And as a result of that, sometimes you believe what you imagine, for however short a space of time, and end up telling lies. You fit events into a story, often a lovely one, events that otherwise might remain unexplained, or sad, or frightening. I know, because I do the same, from time to time. But no, please, let me finish.'

She squeezed his hand tight, then suddenly released it.

'You say you're frightened of people. Well, so am I. And so is everyone, absolutely everyone. We want others to like us, to more than like us, and are genuinely frightened by the knowledge that this often won't happen.

'But as for your being alone, Jim — please, look at me.'

Her hair was bunched up where it had been pressed against the pillow, and half her nightdress collar had got tucked in, underneath. She looked lopsided.

But it was more her determination than these details that Jim saw. She was concentrating hard.

Keeping her gaze on him, she opened her bedside drawer, moved her fingers over various objects, and finally took out a small thing that glittered as it passed beneath the light.

About the size of a fifty-cent piece, yet thicker, and it gleamed gold. She held it out.

'Take it.'

Engraved on one side was *Laura Kavan. First Place, U13 Girls* and on the other were a tennis ball and crossed racquets with *Tacker Bay Tennis Association* around the edge.

'I won it when I was your age, not so many years ago. I want you to keep it, to help you remember something. It's this:

'You aren't alone, Jim. Whatever happens, and for all time, no matter what, you will always have me, for a start. Even when I'm dead, I'll be with you, and that's the truth. Even if you can't see me, or hear me, or hold my hand, I'll be in the air that you breathe, and in the colours that you see. And outside this house, Jim, is a world of people among whom you will certainly, as time goes on, find friends, and more than friends. And then …'

She took his hand and squeezed it.

'And don't think lightly of your imagination, of those worlds that you keep inside your mind. It's a gift, what you have.

'So keep the medallion. Let it remind you of what I've just said. Shh! … Is that Dad's car?'

He could hear nothing, not even the thunder or Paulie's trumpet-playing.

Mrs Liddell spoke quickly.

'Ask Clyde Pharr about Mudlark. He's lived by the Creek all his life. Go now — I'll tell Dad where you're going. And I'll be up tomorrow, at the latest on Monday. Now go, my darling. Hurry.'

He stood up, slipping the medallion into his pocket.

He kissed her cheek, then she reached for the light and turned it off. As he passed through the house he heard the front door open and close. His father.

In his room he sat straight down at his desk, pushed the cage away to give himself room, and wrote, allowing the words to form themselves without thought:

Behemoth turned out to be more savage than anyone had suspected. Until this moment, the boy had thought that he was brave. But this was real. This was no story.

He pushed pen and Journal into the backpack beside the blue blanket and stood up straight.

9

Of the two ways to get from Faraday Avenue to the Creek, the normal one is to go right down Faraday and from there to follow the rusty wire fence of the golf-course to the shops. Here you turn left past the Wintergarden Cinema, past the tennis courts on which Laura Kavan, aged twelve, had won and been presented with her medallion, and there, suddenly before you, lies the Creek. At low tide a stretch of mud with a narrow channel and mangrove trees, at high a spacious river, home to mudlarks who skim the surface, hunting for the insects which, according to Mr Bennet, are their favourite food.

There was a shorter way: directly across the golf-course, where Behemoth lived. Under the rusty fence, into a forest dark even at midday, across fairways and through more forest.

Jim went down the path alongside his house, beneath Paulie's window. Slower music, thoughtful rather than sad, accompanied him. All Mrs Hogan's windows were lit up, and he thought of her bookcases, of the talking cat called Eloise, of the Bible containing the yellow newspaper clipping.

He hardly paused to examine the treetops, gutters and telephone wires for Mudlark. No, he would be at the Creek by now. After a few test flights to warm up his wings, he had flown clear across the golf-course.

Jim halted, nearly at the carport.

Then he retraced his steps, quicker this time, and went straight to the kitchen. All lights off, the house was dark. He opened the cutlery drawer, and as silently as possible reached into the knife compartment, found a handle that he recognised by touch, and slipped the weapon into his jeans pocket.

As he returned to the front garden, a light came on behind him. He ducked into shadow.

Mr Liddell was pulling up the blinds of the spare room, his room. When he had fastened the cord he stood, looking out. With the light behind him he was no more than a silhouette, a thin shadow. Then he turned away, leaving the light on, and Jim ran onto the footpath.

Directly across the road the windows of the Brownscombe house were dark. The white picket fence shone in the glow from the streetlamp.

'Hello,' came a voice which, although soft and tentative, shocked him.

Sam, hair wet and combed, and wearing a shirt with a collar, long trousers, black shoes.

'Oh, hello,' Jim answered, surprised that he felt annoyed.

'How's your mother?' Sam asked.

'She's fine. Should be up tomorrow, or at the latest the day after.'

In the silence that followed, Jim guessed what his friend longed, but was too frightened, to ask. So he answered quickly, to prevent him from speaking.

'Haven't found Mudlark, but I know where he is.'

'Where?'

'Down at the Creek.'

'My father said you could probably buy another mudlark, or some other kind of bird, and Mr Bennet wouldn't mind. Clyde Pharr would know the best sort, he said. He knows all about animals.'

'You told your father about Mudlark?'

'Yes, but —'

'It doesn't matter. Yes, I'll ask Clyde Pharr.'

'When will you go?'

'Now.'

'But it's dark.'

'Only because of the clouds. It isn't night yet.'

'If you leave it till tomorrow, I'll come with you. We have to go out tonight.' Sam dampened his tone. 'To my grandparents'.'

'No, I want to go tonight, I mean, this evening. I want to find Mudlark before he gets pecked to death by the other birds.'

'But —'

'And guess how I'm going.'

'How?'

'Through the golf-course.'

'Golf-course? But Beh —'

'Behemoth? I bet he doesn't exist. We heard a tractor motor starting up, or something.' Although Jim didn't believe this, he liked the brave feeling that saying the words created. So he added, 'It was just a story. One of my stories.'

They were silent.

Jim had never said anything like this before. His 'stories' had always been as real as anything else.

Then he felt tears in his eyes, so he laughed, and turned away. Stepping past Sam, he called out, 'See you tomorrow.'

'Don't go!'

Jim half-turned. 'Don't worry, I'll be all right.'

'Wait till tomorrow, and I'll come.'

And then Jim was striding away, Sam slow and silent behind him, past Sam's house, front doors open, hallway lit up, then into darkness with the foliage from the box trees that lined the road sheltering him from streetlights.

Even though this was the street where he had lived ever since he could remember, Jim didn't know most of the people here. Many of the house windows were dark, which must mean that either they were empty or the inhabitants were in back rooms, or sitting around in darkness.

The largest house in the street was on Jim's side, at the corner with Newcastle Street. Instead of having a back and front garden like the others, it sat in the middle of a triangular block. Tonight, as always, the place stood solemn, dark and empty. Waist-high weeds and grass crowded around. No path led to the front steps. Who had once lived here? Why was it empty now?

Almost certainly, Jim had long ago decided, it was inhabited by ghosts. A whole family of ghosts.

Across the road was the golf-course.

Long, straight Newcastle Street was empty of cars. Along one side were houses and streetlights, opposite was black nothingness. And inside that nothingness …

Jim crossed slowly. His footsteps rang out, although his shoes were rubber-soled. On the golf-course side there was no footpath, only a sandy track between tussocks of grass.

The rusting, eight-foot-high fence was hardly visible in the dark. Beyond was deepest forest. He stopped at a place where the fence sagged out, leaving a foot-high opening at the bottom. This was where he and Sam usually entered — only in the daytime.

Although it was the monster that he most feared, he wasn't only terrified of Behemoth. He reached into his trouser pocket and touched the bone-handled knife he had taken from the cutlery drawer. He had heard that criminals entered the golf-course at night — murderers, drug smugglers, and gangs assembled in the forests and bunkers, pursued each other across fairways, or met to bury or dig up treasure, or to make dangerous plans.

Jim had almost decided to follow Newcastle Street instead, when he found himself, too scared to think about what he was doing, taking off his backpack, glancing left and right to check that there were no cars coming, and crawling beneath the fence.

10

Jim felt as if he were inside his Journal, rather than getting to his feet beside a rough-barked tree in a forest. In his mind, he wrote:

Tonight, Saturday night, was the night of the greatest adventure ever. Deep down, he suspected that this would be his last adventure, that even if he did defeat Behemoth, a beast of fabled savagery, he himself would not survive.

'Are you crazy?' he whispered aloud, and quite sincerely, as he set off down the slope with only cloud-muffled light to show the way.

Impossible to be silent. His shoes crunched twigs and leaves. He went slowly, arms out to protect against branches. A fairway started at the base of the slope. He crouched, perfectly still. Bent nearly double, backpack bouncing on his back, he sprinted across deeply grey grass to the next forest.

Edging between bushes, he knelt on one knee until his breathing was back to normal.

Following a narrow path, he crept even deeper into darkness.

He paused at a fork, and heard a noise so faint yet deep that it was impossible to tell from which direction it was coming.

Growling.

Every last word of the story that Jim had been telling himself vanished. Except for an ache in his stomach, as if he were falling from a great height, he felt nothing.

He was holding his breath, listening. At first the growling was all around him, then it settled on a spot to his right. Without thinking, he sprinted in the opposite direction, along a sandy path, until a tree-root caught his foot and he flew through leaves, trying to regain his balance, before a branch thumped him across the chest. On his back, gasping, he observed that stars were moving in slow circles at the edges of his vision, and that the backpack beneath his head made a comfortable pillow.

Before he could think to roll away from whatever was crashing through the undergrowth after him, the growling became full-throated, and a dark form sprang at him as he lay helpless on the ground. Huge fangs bared themselves inches from his eyes.

Thought and movement were impossible. He merely stared back, then closed his eyes.

'Please, Behemoth,' he heard himself whimper.

He felt hot breath on his neck. The jaws came closer.

But the snarling ceased, and when he next opened his eyes the teeth jumped back, and the clouds parted to allow through just enough moon or left-over sunset to show Mr Stevens' old dog, who had greeted Jim on the way home from school on Friday, as he did on most afternoons.

'Prince?' the boy wondered.

Looking nowhere near as old as he did on the corner of Old South Head Road and Faraday Avenue, the dog stepped closer and licked Jim's cheek.

Laughing with relief, Jim sat up, and patted him.

'Behemoth — Prince! Oh, am I glad it was you.'

After looking around to make sure that there was no other creature nearby, he whispered:

'But what are you doing here, at night?'

He got to his feet, brushing sand from the seat of his pants.

The dog was wagging his tail fiercely.

'I see,' Jim answered, thinking aloud. 'You come here at night, and you pretend. All that barking was just you pretending, wasn't it?'

Prince turned away, tail still wagging, went a little down the path, halted, looked back with ears pricked up, alert.

'I understand,' Jim went on. 'It wrecks the game if I talk about it. Don't worry Prince, I won't say a thing.'

The dog halted again, gazed up at where the moon was glowing behind dense clouds, and let out a long howl. When he had finished, he glanced at Jim.

'Yes,' the boy agreed. 'You're a wolf, and this is a deep, dark forest.'

Jim was about to set off across the next fairway when he heard a scream. It came from behind him, and lasted just as long as Prince's howl. After it came a cry:

'Help!'

High-pitched, the voice of a woman or girl.

Prince had gone, just like that.

When the scream came again, it was deeper, and dragged after it a fearful image of hands pushing against an attacker.

Facing the sound, Jim became coldly aware that he was only twelve years old, and not even strong for that age.

He should run from the golf-course, get the police.

Again came the scream. Briefly, cut off.

He took a step back.

Twelve years old, a voice inside him said.

He thought of his mother, of Paulie and his father, of Sam.

The screaming had stopped.

Perhaps whoever it was had got away. He started to run for Newcastle Street.

'No!' came a shriek.

He halted, turned.

Then he was running through the forest, *towards* the screaming.

He reached the next fairway.

'No!'

It was coming from the forest opposite. He sprinted, feet soundless, pack bouncing on shoulderblades, with the painful draining-away feeling once again in his stomach.

He stopped. Moonlight glistened along the length of a branch.

Just a quarrel, perhaps, between a man and a woman, and when he interrupted them they would both be angry and —

'No!'

He stumbled towards the cry, now amid a noise of twigs and dry leaves that wasn't coming solely from him, but also from up ahead. As he heard another shout — 'No, I said!' — he glimpsed something white, an arm, travelling alone across a gap between trees.

He halted. Not an arm by itself, but whoever owned it was wearing a dark, short-sleeved shirt. Next came a face made entirely of shadow. The arm tugged away. The shadow stumbled.

The slap was followed by a deep voice that Jim immediately recognised.

'Who's there?' it demanded.

It was Andrew Waddell.

'It's me, Jim Liddell. Who have you got there?'

As Jim spoke, he stepped back.

'Jim!' came a cry. 'It's me, Sandra!' She turned to Andrew. 'Let *go* —'

But she was cut off, the breath knocked out of her by Andrew lunging, while still holding on to her hand. His dark head pointed down, and with his free hand he grasped for Jim, but was pulled short by Sandra yanking back.

'Ugh!' he gasped.

He stood upright, glaring. More than a head taller than Jim, he looked much larger, particularly across the shoulders.

He was fourteen or fifteen. Sandra was Jim's age.

'Jim …' Sandra began, trying to use her other hand to loosen Andrew's grip. 'You can't …'

Waddell twisted Sandra's arm so that it went behind her back.

She leant over and reached around uselessly with her free hand.

'Now Jim, come over here,' spoke the boy. 'Come right here, or I cause your girlfriend even more pain.'

Sandra was trying to twist away, but Waddell merely smiled.

As Jim stepped forward, something in the pocket of his shorts bumped against his leg. The knife. He had forgotten it.

He took it out.

…Only to see a fork, a *fork*, in a glint of moonlight. He moved it quickly behind him. He didn't think Waddell had seen.

Then he jumped forward, swinging his arm, aiming for Waddell's side.

Sounding more indignant than hurt, the boy cried out as Jim pushed with the fork, then pushed again.

Jim was sure that it hadn't stuck in, that it couldn't possibly have, yet Waddell stumbled back, clutching his ribs, and Sandra was free.

As Waddell recovered and began to run towards Jim, Jim again advanced, just as threateningly, and this time it was Waddell who stepped back first.

'I'll get you!' he shouted, glaring at Jim, one hand pressed to his side.

'Come on!' Sandra tugged at Jim's arm.

As they moved away, and Waddell began to follow them, loud barking cut off the boy's next shout, and amid a noisy breaking of twigs and flurry of sand and leaves, Prince landed on the path, paws wide apart. After glancing at Jim as though to make sure that he was watching, he faced Waddell and snarled. And now Prince really did look fierce. His fur had risen along his neck, and saliva dripped from black lips that quivered with rage.

A single leaf lay on the back of the dog's neck, on a patch of grey fur.

Waddell retreated.

'Wait, Prince, come on …' he began to soothe.

Encouraged, the dog growled and barked more loudly.

Jim and Sandra ran for the fairway, then across the grass, through the next forest, and up to the fence, not caring how much noise they made. They scrambled beneath, then crossed Newcastle Street, until they were opposite the haunted house in Faraday Avenue.

Simultaneously, they turned to look back at the golf-course. Their shoulders touched, they stood so close to one another.

'Are you all right?' Jim asked, his voice sounding terribly loud.

Sandra was rubbing her wrist.

Her hair stuck up at the back, half of it out of the ponytail, rubberband hanging. She pulled this off, shook out her hair, then caught it together in one hand while the other slipped the band back in place.

'I don't know why I do things sometimes,' she said. 'Now I have to get home. I'll see you later.'

'Oh,' she added, with a laugh, 'thank you for rescuing me. But Jim ...' She looked into his eyes. 'What were you doing in the golf-course, with a fork? Look, you're still holding it.'

He raised his hand. The metal glinted green. He doubted that it had even torn Waddell's shirt, or bruised him. But Waddell must have thought it was a knife.

'I'm on my way to see Clyde Pharr,' he answered.

He told her about Mudlark, and how both his mother and Mick Ryan had advised him to go and see Clyde.

When he had finished, Sandra reached for the fork. 'May I?'

He gave it to her. She turned it over carefully, like an archaeologist examining a just-unearthed piece of ancient treasure.

Then she used it to point down the road.

'Mick Ryan ... did you know that he killed someone, once, a long time ago? Got into a fight, and murdered a man. Went to prison, and must have got out before we were born, because he's been living where he is now at least since then.'

Jim remembered Mick's anger this afternoon. The house itself was barely visible in the shadows beyond a streetlight.

'Can I keep this?' Sandra held up the fork.

'Yes.'

'Well, see you later.'

As she walked quickly away from him, down Faraday Avenue, Jim wondered if it wasn't too late to visit Clyde Pharr.

If Clyde's windows were dark, he could always just come home again.

So Jim crossed Albermarle Avenue and passed the sandstone gates of Tacker Bay Public School where, yesterday morning, Mr Harding had asked him if his parents allowed him to attend school looking the way he did.

Did his mother and father know about Mick Ryan?

'So you're the police, out to catch a jailbird,' Mick
had said.

Had Mick had escaped from jail, or been chased
and captured?

11

Jim went down Newcastle Street, past the golf-course, Wintergarden Cinema, the tennis courts and St Xavier's Church. He cut through a pedestrian path between a fish-and-chip shop and a grocery store that took him all the way to the Reserve. Beyond benches and grass was the Creek, with its jetties and boats. The water reflected house and verandah lights in long lines that were always being broken and repaired by gentle waves.

On the other side of the Creek was the National Park, with the mangroves where the mudlarks lived. The birds who had, more than a year ago, tried to kill Mudlark.

Jim took a deep breath. Yes, Mudlark was here. He was sure of it.

Clyde Pharr's backyard was a rocky mountainside. He lived further down the Creek than anyone in Tacker Bay, and his front garden went right to the high-water mark.

Everyone in Tacker Bay, at least once, and usually more than once, came to see Clyde Pharr's garden.

He had begun it many years ago, on his return from the war. After months in hospital recovering from wounds, he had settled in Tacker Bay rather than in Nalmo, across the Bay, where he had grown up.

From the mountainside he had brought down rocks and stones. Using gravel, sand and galvanised iron drainage pipes, he had constructed above-ground and below-ground canals that kept fresh water flowing into the ponds. Here lilies flourished, with orchids in the shadows beneath ferns and moon-flower bushes. Tiny-petalled daisies traced out paths, then trailed away between rocks.

Next, Clyde added mountains, forests and fields. He made suspension bridges of wire and sheet-iron, and others from miniature planks, like the rattling ones in the country. He built roads and paths, all to scale, and in this miniature landscape he placed painted figures of people, animals, cars, even trucks and buses, and a scattering of cottages complete with tiny front and backyards.

So Clyde Pharr's garden had become a world in itself. Its cool shadows and sunlit heights, cliffs and deep lakes, easily made up for the fact that nothing except for the plants and the surface of the water ever moved.

When a bird — often a mudlark — settled by a lake to bathe or drink, so lifelike were its surroundings that it was the bird who seemed to have wandered in from a fantasy world, not the motionless fisherman beside it.

A dry riverbed with soft grass growing on its banks curled through the garden, serving as a path from the gate to the front door.

Tonight, Jim halted at a detail that he had never noticed before. At the shore of the broadest river — about nine inches wide — a party of soldiers were standing to attention. There had always been soldiers in the landscape, mingling with civilians around a barbecue, or fishing by the lake, or with suitcases at a bus-stop ready to return to camp, but Jim had never before noticed a group as large as this.

Yet Clyde did alter parts of his garden from time to time. Mountains toppled and were smoothed into plains. Rivers flooded, transforming flowerbeds into marshlands, or became filled with silt and stones to make a containing wall for a new lake.

Yet why were these soldiers here, and standing to attention in a straight line at the bank of a river that, tonight, was pure black?

• • •

'Jim Liddell! Come up, please. I've been expecting you,' came a soft voice from the verandah.

Clyde Pharr was halfway down the steps, wearing a short-sleeved shirt with a collar, tucked into baggy shorts that made his legs look even thinner than they were. He raised his hand in a wave of greeting, and his fingers trembled as he lowered it again.

For as long as Jim had known him, Clyde had been old, even older than Mrs Hogan. The breeze caught wisps of his white hair, and lifted them almost straight up as he came down the stairs. Near the hairline above his left eye was an angular dent as deep as a thumbnail. This, a limping walk, and perhaps the tremor in his fingers, were legacies of his war-time injuries.

'Your father telephoned to say that you might be coming. Come in, come in.' He lightly patted Jim's shoulder, while looking up at the sky. 'You know, I think we're in for a storm. Can you smell the electricity?'

He cast a quick look over the garden, then climbed the steps.

A light with a shade that left the ceiling in darkness hung low over a full-sized billiard table, crowded with balls. A cue lay across one corner. Spread across the arm of a chair was a book, cover facing up. On the bookcase was a single framed photograph of a group of old-fashioned looking soldiers.

Jim had never seen this photo before, not in all his visits here with his mother — to play billiards or to drop in seedlings, fertiliser, or a present of something to eat.

Clyde went straight to the cue rack, got down the triangular frame, and racked up the balls. Upon entering Clyde's place, it was assumed that you would like to play, even if you only had time for a few shots.

Jim took his usual cue, a three-quarter one with triangles of deeper-coloured wood inlaid at the thicker end.

Clyde placed the white ball on its spot, and flipped a coin.

'Tails,' called Jim, as usual.

'Tails it is. You break.'

Playing, you could talk, but while actually shooting it was customary to be silent. Times spent here with his mother had taught Jim that the intervals between shots could last for ages. When he had been little he had often fallen asleep in one of the huge, comfortable armchairs, while Clyde and his mother talked away.

As Jim accidentally sank a red into a middle pocket, thunder rumbled.

'There we are,' Clyde proclaimed, advancing towards the white. 'A storm. Wind too. Can you hear?'

Clyde owned a radio and record player, but neither was on. Into the silence came the moan of wind through the National Park forest, then more thunder. He went to the windows and pulled back the gauze curtains just as lightning flashed, dispelling the room's cosy light and for an instant making every object stand out as if carved from marble.

Clyde glanced at his garden without looking at all worried, and stepped back from the window.

'How is Laura, Jim?'

Meditatively, he approached the table, as though this next shot was one that would require much thought.

He never referred to Mrs Liddell as 'your mother', always as 'Laura'. He had always been her best friend, it seemed to Jim. Ages ago, he had been a friend of her father's.

'She's fine. Getting up tomorrow, or the day after at the latest.'

Clyde rubbed his chin, studying the position of the balls.

'Good. Good. Well, you tell her, will you, to come down here as soon as she feels up to it. I've made several changes to the garden, and have several others in mind. I'd like her opinion on them.'

'Sure, I will.'

Jim found himself half-kneeling to study the photograph of soldiers. Was his grandfather among them? The men were arranged in tiers, like in a class photo.

The balls clicked as Clyde made his first shot,

successful from the soft noise of a ball falling into a pocket-net.

The soldiers' faces were young, looking not much older than Year Twelve boys, some perhaps even younger. He thought he could make out Clyde, at the back and second from the left. The same thoughtful eyes, as though he was already imagining the garden that he would one day create.

His hair was dark, and there was no dent on his forehead.

Startling Jim, because he hadn't heard him approach, Clyde picked up the photograph.

'Taken six months before I came home for good,' he mentioned in his quiet voice, as rain drummed on the corrugated iron roof.

'It was in the bottom of a suitcase until last week, when I took it out and put it in this frame. I want to show it to Laura. See, there. That's your grandfather, your mother's father.'

He pointed to a young man with black hair shaved away at the sides, which made his ears seem to stick out. He had a pale face and a broad, happy grin.

It looked as if he had thought of something funny to tell his friends the moment the photographer finished his work.

'All of them except for your grandfather and me died nine weeks after this photo was taken. Yes, nine weeks. We had landed on a beach, and were digging in, when a shell exploded right among us. Your grandfather lost a hand and a lung, and died twelve years later. I spent some time in hospital, and was fine after that.'

Clyde had not told Jim this story before, had never mentioned the war.

He placed the photo back on the bookcase.

'Consequently, only two of those twenty-one boys finished growing up. None of the rest started a family, pursued a career, grew old, and so on and so forth.'

Clyde began to line up a shot. Dissatisfied with the angle, he straightened.

'Your father tells me that you've lost a mudlark.'

'Yes.'

'And that's why you came here — at least one

reason — to ask my advice on how to get the bird back?'

'Yes.'

By now, rain was overflowing the gutters. Jim heard it splashing. What would this weather do to the delicate garden just outside? Yet Clyde seemed unconcerned by the storm.

'This mudlark, what is his or her name?'

'It's a male, called Mudlark.'

'I see. And how long had Mudlark been in a cage?'

'About a year. Mr Bennet, my teacher, found him near here, being attacked by other mudlarks.'

Clyde shook his head.

'You know what? Here you are, a guest, and I haven't offered you anything to eat or drink. I've got sausage rolls, fresh baked, that only need heating, and a whole box of fruit. You have your turn, while I get the food. Then we'll continue our talk about Mudlark.'

When Clyde had gone, Jim went to the window to see how the garden was making out in the storm.

Curtain pulled back, he was startled to find himself inches from his grandfather's face.

But of course it was just that his own reflection had reminded him of his grandfather in the photo on Clyde's bookcase.

'I haven't been there for years,' Clyde began, raising his voice above the wind and rain. They were seated in armchairs, plates on knees, eating. 'But down the very end of the Creek, where it gets hardly wider than a billiard table, there's a cave where the mudlarks go when they're about to die. The entrance is on the left as you go down. Just after a flat place, with the ruins of a stone farmhouse in a field of tall grass. If Mudlark were seriously injured, that's where he'd go.'

A gust of rain made the windows tremble in their frames.

'You can borrow my canoe, under the house. You know that. Whenever you want. You could bring Mudlark back, and take him to the vet. There's one here, near the Estuary. On the other hand, you might decide that it's better for Mudlark to stay there. He might have decided that it's time for him to die.'

'But it's my fault,' Jim protested. 'If he dies, then I'll have caused it by letting him out of the cage.'

Clyde had placed a cloth napkin on the arm of both their chairs. He used his to wipe his lips, fingers trembling slightly. Then he took a sip of raspberry cordial so cold that the glass was already coated with droplets of condensation.

'Your fault,' he echoed. 'Excuse me if I disagree with you. Mudlark took the decision to leave his cage. Who can tell, exactly, what motives lie behind another creature's actions? The older I get, the less I understand. Come, let's finish our game. I see that you've left a pretty tough set-up. Well, I'll see what I can do.'

As a young man, Jim's mother had told him, Clyde had defeated Eddie Duchamp, the Tacker Bay National, and ultimately World, Billiards Champion. Few, therefore, would be capable of defeating Clyde. He concentrated so hard on each shot, Jim gained the impression that he was playing not against him, a boy who hardly even knew how to play, but against an imaginary, great opponent, perhaps Eddie Duchamp himself.

Although Clyde never faked a shot to lose a point on purpose, he nevertheless tried only the most difficult angles, those that to any but a true champion would have been impossible. And when he failed he gave a sigh, and a little shake of his head, as though in appreciation of his opponent's skill and the closeness of the contest.

He usually won. When he had sunk the black and ended the game, he shook Jim's hand.

'Good game. Close.'

Outside, the wind pushed at TV antennas, making them rattle, and howled through electricity wires. Whitecaps hurried across the Creek, and a whole fleet of little boats tossed and twisted at their moorings.

Jim wondered that Clyde hadn't gone onto the verandah, or at least to the window overlooking it, to check how his garden was getting on in the storm.

He was making for the windows himself, to see, when Clyde said:

'You can stay the night if you like. I have a spare room. Then you can take the canoe up the Creek first thing in the morning, if the weather's cleared, which I expect it will have.'

As Jim began to help get the balls out of the pockets, he wondered how Clyde could have gone to bed in an empty house, so much alone, for so many years.

'Thank you, but I don't know. My parents …'

'You can ring them, if you like.'

'Yes,' Jim said quickly, envisaging just how empty his own house would seem, with his mother's door closed, father asleep in front of the TV, Paulie either practising or asleep, and the birdcage on the map of the world.

'Yes, I'll ring them. I'd like to stay, if that's all right.'

He dialled his own number, and listened to the ring, ring, ring. No chance of waking his mother: the phone was the other side of the house, in the dining room. TV sounds must be hiding the ringing from his father, and Paulie's door would be shut, with the mattress across it.

'No answer? It's pretty late. Anyway, your father said it mightn't be a bad idea if you stayed here, because of the storm. The bed in the spare room is all made up. There's a spare toothbrush — the one still in its packet — in the bathroom cabinet, behind the mirror. I'm going to bed now. But *you* don't have to, of course. You're welcome to try any of my books.' He gestured at the bookcases. 'Well, goodnight then.'

The spare room had a single bed against a wall, a dressing table with tilt-mirror, wardrobe, desk, a chair, and a bedside table with reading lamp. A rug at the centre felt soft against Jim's bare feet.

Still in the T-shirt and jeans that he had worn all day, Jim pulled the sheets and blankets over himself and placed the book that he had chosen on the bedside table. He had not felt tired while choosing the book, but now his hand was almost too heavy to lift as he reached to turn off the bedside light.

Yet he didn't want to go to sleep just yet. The events of the day tumbled through his mind. Mudlark, Sam, Sandra, Mrs Hogan, Mick Ryan, and his mother in the darkened bedroom that smelt of medicines. He thought of tonight in the golf-course. Sandra had asked for the fork. Why? And Waddell? Had *he* been nothing but an imaginary monster, like Behemoth?

He pulled back the covers and placed his feet on the soft rug. He would get a glass of water.

To reach the kitchen he had to pass the doorway to the billiard room. The light over the table was still on. What had the storm done to Clyde's garden? Wanting to delay his return to bed, he made for the window, silently, on bare feet, halting when he heard a ghostly creak of hinges.

Pushed by the wind, the front door had yawned open. The fly-screen rattled.

Clyde must have forgotten to shut it.

Jim caught the door as it started to swing back, and noticed, a light in the garden, hazy through the screen.

Stepping closer, he saw a figure in a yellow, hooded raincoat. It was Clyde, judging by the curve of the shoulders, the skinny legs.

Jim stepped onto the verandah. It was raining steadily, though not as hard as before, and the wind had died down. The entire garden was lit by a spotlight, and seemed to Jim not to have been damaged. A few twigs and leaves floated on the largest lake, and some of the flowers were bowed over, but that was all.

Seeing Jim on the steps, Clyde straightened.

When Jim reached the bottom, the rain struck his face and bare arms. Clyde gave a quick shake of his head, like someone about to apologise for something. Cupped together, his hands were black with mud.

'Jim, you'd better go back. You'll get wet.'

It wasn't just mud on his fingers, Clyde was carrying something.

The rain was washing mud from a whole tangle of objects in Clyde's hands. Jim made out a tiny pair of boots, attached to legs, a face … The toy soldiers, the ones he had seen as he had come through the garden this evening.

Rain dribbled from Clyde's hood onto these figures, and Jim recalled the photograph on the bookcase. Except for his mother's father, who had lived for twelve years longer, and Clyde himself, all twenty-one soldiers had died in a single explosion.

The old gardener raised his eyes and smiled.

'Yes, I take care of them,' he explained.

PART THREE

PART THREE

12

Weak light entered the bedroom. Jim put his feet on the rug and pulled on socks and shoes.

There was a note on the kitchen table, with a plastic cordial bottle full of water on one corner to prevent it from blowing away.

Dear Jim,

Gone shopping. Back soon. The canoe is under the house, on the driveway side, if you want to make an early start. Take this bottle of water with you. I'll be getting *bacon and eggs, but there's cereal in the cupboard above the fridge.*

Clyde.

A clock on the stove said a quarter to nine.

Mudlark! Breakfast could wait.

Jim got his backpack, containing blue blanket-net and Journal, and added the water bottle to it. He went to the phone in the billiard room, started to dial his home number, then changed his mind, and dialled Sam's instead.

'Sam? Guess what? I'm at Clyde's place. I'm about to go up the Creek, to find Mudlark.'

'Do you want me to come? I'll run. I'll be there in a couple of minutes.'

Without knowing why, Jim found himself saying, 'No, no …'

Suddenly the reasons why he had wanted to ring Sam — to tell him about Behemoth and Waddell, for instance — disappeared. Instead, he felt frightened. Frightened for Mudlark.

'No, no, I'll be back soon. I'll see you later.'

He hung up and went out by the back door.

The canoe was a single-seater, made of fibreglass painted white. It rested on planks covered by strips of carpet, between two of the pylons that raised the house about a metre above the ground.

The rain had stopped, but the air was cooler than yesterday, and the sky was the colour of corrugated iron. Jim pulled the canoe out, reached one arm over it and a hand underneath. Light to drag, it was heavy to carry.

The gate was open. He took long, staggering steps down the driveway, and hardly gave the garden a glance.

Struggling against gusts of wind, he crossed the grassy Reserve. The tide was halfway out. He took off his shoes, pushed them beneath the seat, folded his jeans up to his knees, picked up the canoe again and stepped onto sand, then into colder, silty mud that oozed between his toes.

As soon as he could he lowered the canoe and pushed it until the water was halfway up to his knees. He climbed in.

As he paddled for the channel, a boat with an outboard motor chugged past.

'Morning!' shouted a man at the bow and a woman at the tiller, waving.

A sailing boat, further up-creek, was tacking towards the mangroves.

Jim waited until the waves from the motorboat had passed, then began to paddle again.

Immediately after its first bend, both the Creek and its channel widened. The water was pale brown from all the earth washed in by last night's rain.

Occasionally he rested, paddle crossways, the wind from over the mangroves gently pushing him towards the Tacker Bay side.

At one of these rests he took a long drink from the water bottle, then got out his Journal and wrote:

The voyage of exploration had to be attempted by one person, alone.

'Jim! Jim Liddell!' came a voice that caused him to stuff Journal and pen hurriedly into the pack as if someone were peering over his shoulder.

A little sailing boat was heading straight for him with a small man at the stern, one hand on the tiller and the other waving. Sleeves rolled up, his shirt was sky-blue and his arms and face were tanned golden brown.

It was Mr Harding, the deputy-headmaster.

Grinning, he continued to wave, and just as it seemed as if he would cut the canoe in half, the sail sagged, Mr Harding ducked as the boom swung across, and as soon as the sail filled again he was whisked towards the mangroves, calling out as he vanished:

'Lovely day, Jim. Bye!'

'Bye!'

Jim continued paddling, wind and water suddenly silent after the departure of Mr Harding.

Shoals of garfish rushed ahead, churning the surface. From time to time a larger fish, a flathead or blackfish, would stir and with two slow waves of its tail move out of the way.

Then the Creek narrowed to be no wider than a three-lane road, and tall grass came right down to its edge. Not long afterwards, it began to wind so that it was rarely possible to see further than ten metres ahead. In the upper branches of high trees, the wind sighed and rustled, making the only sounds in what seemed to be an empty world.

Jim paddled slowly, through nearly motionless water. After passing through a gap hardly a foot wide between the bank and a fallen tree, he looked up. On a low branch, close enough for him to reach out and touch it, was a mudlark.

He held his breath. Water dripped from the paddle. Before he could think that this bird looked tame enough to be Mudlark, it was joined by another.

Both contemplated Jim, then flew back over the boy's head, and as he turned to watch, another pair joined them, and in a single movement they all swerved one way, then the other, before vanishing into the shadows beyond the grass.

When Jim turned back, a sudden speck of blue caught his eye, skimming so quickly across the water that he couldn't see what it was until it halted on a branch, glanced at Jim and gave a flurry of little impatient shakes of its head.

'So much to do!' the kingfisher seemed to be insisting. 'So little time! Come! Hurry!'

It rushed ahead, and again halted on a branch.

It seemed to be showing him the way.

Jim paddled cautiously, though, on the lookout for snags and submerged rocks.

Around the next bend the kingfisher veered off, to settle on a pile of grey stones. The ruins of a wall, fireplace and chimney rose no more than a few feet above tall grass. The kingfisher hopped to the chimney. As the boy watched, entranced by the silence of this place, a group of mudlarks sped overhead, five or six of them. Tumbling and rolling, calling to one another, they separated into two groups as they approached the kingfisher and the chimney, before reuniting on the other side and disappearing into the forest.

Sunlight from a break in the clouds turned grass-stalks to gold, and lit up each leaf from within. For an instant the kingfisher on the chimney might have been a gem of blueness, the essence of a cloudless sky brought down to Earth, a colour nearly too bright to look at.

And now, as Jim neared his goal, the paddle grew heavy, and he began to be afraid of what he might find.

He recalled Mudlark in his cage, beside Mr Bennet's desk, and how content the bird had been with a whole class of children for company and a window nearby. And then he thought of the empty cage on his desk at home. If he found Mudlark dead or dying, it would of course be his own fault for taking the risk, however small it might have seemed, of letting him out of the cage.

Now the Creek was hardly wider than a footpath. The kingfisher flashed off into forest darkness.

The water was black and still. Across its surface skated long-legged insects. A frog croaked. And from all around came the rhythmical soughing of the wind in the uppermost branches.

A voice within him warned: *You have gone too far. Too far and too deep. You will never get back.*

Yet he continued paddling, neither helped nor hindered by any current from the black water.

The trees met overhead. As the Creek narrowed to be hardly wider than the canoe itself, and the grass either side was replaced by trees and thorny blackberry bushes, he noticed a hole a few metres up from the bank, beneath a grey-green, overhanging rock. The entrance to the cave.

Jim laid the paddle down, reached out, grabbed a branch and pulled the canoe to the bank.

The hole was round, its edges flecked with dried mud. Reddish-gold light, the colour of an autumn leaf, moved against a wall inside.

Jim's shoulders and arms ached. Never before had he paddled so far, and he still had the return journey to make. He was hungry too.

He could turn back now. Wouldn't it upset the mudlarks, for him to enter their graveyard?

Yet he couldn't make himself believe it. This place was too powerful to be affected by anything that he might do. He was only here at all, he sensed, because it had allowed him to come.

And so, moving slowly, he unzipped his backpack and got out the blue blanket. As he gripped a branch and stepped onto the bank, it occurred to him how remote his own world was, his mother and father and Paulie at home, Sandra across the road, Sam, Mick, Mrs Hogan, Clyde, school. That faraway place now seemed miniature, like Clyde's garden.

The mud around the entrance to the cave was smooth to the touch. He leant in.

But this was merely an entrance-hall, the start of a tunnel. The floor was smooth and clean. As he crawled inside, going first up and then down a gradual slope, the tree sounds faded until he could hear his own beating heart.

He crawled some more, then found himself in a cave bigger than his living room at home. The ceiling was twice as high. He stood up. Something moved, above. A blue sparkle — the kingfisher perched on one of the branches that bristled around a light-filled opening.

As Jim stepped into the centre, a perfume arose from around his bare, mud-caked feet that reminded him of his mother's bedroom. He thought he was treading on old leaves, but as the light passed across them he made out the red and blue petals of wildflowers.

From floor to ceiling, set into the clay walls, were shelves, and on at least half of these lay delicate clusters of bones, bird skeletons, wings and legs tucked in. Jim stepped through the petals, making more of the gentle perfume rise. The kingfisher watched him carefully.

The light shifted.

Among the shadows, Jim made out his mother, pushing herself higher in her bed, oxygen mask in her lap, and when she was sitting up she reached out with both her arms for him. Her mouth opened as she silently called his name. Her dark eyes were open wide. She looked frightened.

Then the light grew brighter, and the rows of shadowy shelves returned, with their huddled bird-skeletons.

For a while his arms and legs were too heavy for him to move. It had only been shadows, trees, clouds, moving above the hole in the roof. It didn't mean anything. He recalled how his mother had consoled him, yesterday afternoon, over the loss of

Mudlark, and over the other things that he had told her. He had felt hopeless and weak, as if he hardly existed, but his mother had driven that feeling away.

He walked around the cave, the blue blanket over his shoulder.

Mudlark was not here. Guarded by the blue kingfisher, there was nothing here but bones, nothing but death.

Yet not frightening, cold death, as he had often imagined it. No, here it was warm, and ancient, and wrapped around with reddish-golden light.

Afterwards, thinking back, he had no idea how long he remained in the cave. It could have been a minute or two, or as long as an hour. When he left, a cold wind was pushing the treetops in one direction, then another, unable to make up its mind.

Helped by the tide, he paddled back up the Creek, now empty of fishing and sailing boats, to Clyde's place.

13

Canoe back under the house, Jim stood in the driveway and hosed mud from his feet. The house was empty. He got a slice of bread from the kitchen, and as he came out eating it, Clyde drove up in his old blue Morris. Barely visible through a windscreen crowded with reflections of clouds, he raised a hand in greeting and got out, not turning off the motor.

'Want a lift home?' He brought out a handkerchief, turned away and blew his nose.

Jim was sitting on a rock, tugging shoes over wet feet.

'Oh, no, thank you, I want to walk.'

'Are you sure?' The light caught the edge of the dent in Clyde's forehead.

'Yes, thank you.'

Clyde nodded at the house.

'I rang your father. Told him you'd be back soon. Sure you don't want a lift?'

'Sure, and thank you for the water bottle.' He handed this over, then laced up his shoes and put on the backpack containing blanket and Journal.

Clyde hadn't asked, but Jim found himself saying, 'I didn't find Mudlark.'

Then Clyde came over, and pulled Jim to him, so that the boy stumbled a bit, and gave him a clumsy, unpractised hug.

'You be sure to come and see me again soon.'

'I will, Clyde.' Awkwardly, surprised, he stepped back.

'Promise? Soon?'

'Yes.'

Clyde turned away, and as Jim set off down the drive, Clyde called out:

'Soon, I mean it. I need some help with the garden. Hate to admit it, but I'm getting old. I pay top wages, you know.'

'Yes, I will!' Jim waved, straightening the backpack straps. He walked as quickly as he could down the dirt road and then along the path that emerged beside the grocery store.

Here, at a bus-stop, he sat on a bench, tugged his Journal from the backpack and wrote:

Just when he thought his journey was over, he discovered a freezing rock. No, not a rock, but a chunk of ice as tall as a ten-storey building. Beyond this was more ice, mountains of ice all the way to the sky.

He set off again, swinging his arms and walking as quickly as he could to keep warm.

Climbing a mountain all by yourself, the greatest obstacle would be the silence. Maybe eagles, for whom great heights were nothing, would offer encouragement. He pictured a wise old eagle, with feathery grey eyebrows, inviting him to his nest for a cup of tea.

He laughed at the thought. In his imagination, this old eagle, who would have a whispery voice like Clyde's, was already his friend. Perhaps he would bring him to life tonight, in bed.

Flat, grey clouds still covered the sky.

Tomorrow he would return to school, carrying an empty birdcage.

Grass whipped at his ankles. He noticed a trembling, sagging fence.

The golf-course.

He was nearly home.

Behemoth had turned out to be Prince, Mr Stevens' old dog. And Andrew Waddell would never frighten him again.

He was exhausted.

He crossed empty Newcastle Street.

Clyde had held toy soldiers in his hands, last night. Jim turned quickly away from this memory.

His back and shoulders ached from paddling, and a blister on his right hand stung.

• • •

Although hardly walking at all — just taking a few
steps now and then, and stopping to adjust the
straps of the backpack or to rub his hand where it
hurt — Jim soon found himself opposite the
Brownscombes' place with its picket fence and
concrete driveway still damp from when Mr
Brownscombe had washed his stationwagon, at half-
past ten this morning. Was Sandra in her room, still
with his fork?

As he drew level, the door opened, and Mrs
Brownscombe waved. She was wearing jeans and a
blue jumper that must have belonged to her
husband, because it nearly reached her knees and
was bunched up above her wrists.

He waved back.

His father's car was in the carport.

Jim leant against the brick column beside his gate
and closed his eyes. He felt that he didn't have the
strength to climb the single step that led to the path
of sandstone stepping-stones that his father had laid,

soon after they had moved to this house so many years ago. He could hardly remember that far back. One of his earliest memories was of the front yard on a sunny day, a sprinkler sending up whirls of drops to fall not on grass or flowers but on grass seed and black mud.

He opened the gate, climbed the step. His throat felt tight, his chest ached. 'Perhaps you're sick,' he told himself. 'Too sick to go to school tomorrow.' But he couldn't believe it. 'It's this day. The wind and the clouds. And you're hungry and tired.'

He hadn't brought his key. He started to go around the back, but somehow the thought of the side path, and of the empty courtyard, deterred him. Anyway, his father was home.

Something made him turn around, just before he raised and lowered the knocker.

Lawn, path, wall, letterbox … Mrs Brownscombe was no longer in her garden.

He lowered the knocker once, as softly as he could.

The door opened almost immediately.

'Jim!' It was Sonya Hogan, from next door. 'Jim, come inside.'

Her grey-black hair was half pinned up and half falling over her face.

'Tony?' She stepped back and faced the spare room doorway. 'Tony, Jim's home.'

The hallway was dark. His mother's lovely, blue-green door lay in shadow.

'Tony …' Sonya called again, but before she had finished, Jim stepped forward, about to ask what was going on, to see his father crossing the spare room towards him, overhead light off but bedside lamp on.

The phone rang.

'I'll get it.' Raising both hands to her glasses, Sonya jogged away. She had on slippers that covered her toes but left her pale heels bare.

The skin around his father's eyes was pink, the rest of his face paler than Jim had ever seen it. A clear droplet hung from the tip of his nose. As he wiped this away with the back of a hand, he took Jim's arm gently in the other, and led him into the spare room.

'Over here.' He steered his younger son to a chair at the foot of the bed. 'Please, sit down.'

Mr Liddell sat on the bed. Their knees nearly touched. He took a deep breath.

'Jim, Mum died this afternoon. She …'

And that was as much as he could say for now. His shoulders shook. He leant right over, and covered his face with his hands.

As light vanished altogether outside Nine Faraday Avenue, inside it became timid. Overhead bulbs refused to send their glow much lower than the ceiling, while the illumination from lamps stubbornly remained in corners.

'No!' Jim cried. He grabbed his father's wrists. 'She was fine! She was going to get up, today or tomorrow. She was getting better!'

Mr Liddell was shaking his head.

'No, Jim. That was what you told yourself. We all tried to tell you the truth, but you wouldn't listen. Whenever we started, you changed the subject. You talked about something else and hurried away.

160

She tried to tell you herself. No, Jim, she came home to die. She didn't want to stay in the hospital any longer.'

'But I spoke to her yesterday. She said she was going to be *fine*.'

'Jim, she's hardly been conscious for a moment since she got home.'

'But I did!'

Mr Liddell raised his head, and in his eyes was a look of such sadness that Jim fell immediately silent, and went to hug him.

But his father held out a hand to halt him.

'What you did, believing that Mum was all right, if I could have done it, I would have. But I don't have your power of imagination. A gift, Jim, believe me, it's a gift, what you have. Don't ever think of it as anything else. Never believe anyone, if they say that it isn't. But like every gift, it has its price.'

14

Paulie had joined them, trumpet dangling from a single finger as though he was just about to let go of it forever. Together they went into their mother's room, but Jim could hardly do more than glance at the bed, and at the utterly silent figure beneath the covers, face not so much peaceful (as Jim had read or heard somewhere about the faces of the dead) as empty.

Later — he couldn't have said how much later — Sonya had an arm around his shoulder, and was suggesting that he take a shower.

'Mud,' she whispered. 'Your legs, arms.' She handed him a towel, and as he moved towards the bathroom he thought over what his father had told him. While he showered, amid the steam appeared faces from the past couple of days: Mr Harding and Mr Bennet, Sonya, Mick Ryan, Sam, Sandra, and Clyde.

Yes, they had all known. They all had known that his mother was dying, that there had been no hope.

No hope.

'Jim, are you okay in there?' came Sonya's voice.

'I'll be out in a moment.'

'No, no … only asking. No hurry.'

He dried himself, and only when, wrapped in a towel, he had opened the door, did he realise that he had left the shower on. He turned it off, and went to his room to dress.

Mudlark's empty cage on the map of the world was nothing but wires, a bowl containing water, another containing seed. Yet it stung him, seeing it, to think that he had been so worried about an escaped bird while his mother …

He concentrated on getting dressed.

He smelt food, something cooking, and shook his head with disgust to realise that he was hungry.

He pulled on jeans and laced up shoes.

Without knowing quite how he had got there, he found himself on the footpath outside his house, fully dressed and wondering if he had imagined yesterday's conversation with his mother.

It was almost funny. She had been dying, and he had complained to her about Mudlark and how unhappy he was. 'I'm frightened …' he had said. And although he longed to believe that he really had spoken to her before heading off to Clyde's place, and that she had said what he remembered her saying, he decided that he must have imagined this too.

'Every gift has its price,' his father had said.

The streetlights had come on. A droplet from his still-wet hair slid down his forehead.

Very slowly, he wandered down the street. He felt dizzy for a moment, and held on to a wall. Yes, he was extremely hungry, had eaten hardly anything all day. Soon he would go home, or his father would be worried. He would eat, go to bed, and tomorrow morning he would wake up. He would go to school, or perhaps since there were only three days left of the term — of the year — he would not go, on account of his mother's death.

'No!' he cried out. He kicked at the grass by the footpath, then punched a tree-trunk. 'No! No! No!' And then he was sitting on the grass, crying.

'No!' he said over and over.

A car turned into Faraday Avenue. He stood up quickly, brushed a forearm over his eyes, rubbed his bruised knuckles, and set off purposefully, as though he knew where he was going.

As the car approached, invisible behind the glow of its headlights, he turned away and found himself looking at the paling fence of the abandoned house on the corner of Newcastle Street and Faraday Avenue. For as long as anyone could remember, this house had been empty.

Yet the gate opened at his touch. No path, only knee-high grass and weeds. He sat down at the top of the verandah steps. Except for a sighing from the trees in the golf-course, the wind was silent. The moon appeared through a tear in the fast-moving clouds.

Jim walked across the verandah and back again. His footsteps resounded.

'So where are you?' he asked aloud.

No, he couldn't have imagined speaking to her yesterday. Yet his father was right — he had blocked from his mind just how sick she had been.

'If it's at all possible,' she had said yesterday, 'and even if it's not, I'll always be with you.'

'Are you here now?' he asked softly. 'Yes,' he answered for her. 'Everywhere. You're everywhere now, all around.'

As he turned back towards the gate, he noticed a figure there. It was Clyde. Behind him was the little blue Morris.

'Hello. Want a lift back?' came the old man's gentle voice.

• • •

Jim woke early. The light was barely grey. It was some time before the sun would rise. His window was still open at the top.

Monday. School. Mudlark. And then he remembered, and sat suddenly upright, put his feet on the floor, and doubled over at the ache in his stomach.

He stayed like this for a while, rocking back and forth, then headed off to the kitchen to get some breakfast.

On the kitchen bench, by the telephone, lay five of his mother's history books. An ambulance had come last night and taken away her body. The funeral was tomorrow. Jim rested his hands on the books for a moment, then returned to his room.

On the floor, forgotten, was the backpack that he had taken with him yesterday, while hunting for Mudlark. He unzipped it and took out the Journal. He went to drop it into the waste-paper bin, but placed it on his desk instead. All those stories that he had made up.

He pulled out the loosely woven baby-blanket that he had hoped to use as a net. He picked leaves and twigs from it and placed them carefully in the bin. Part of it was smudged with dirt. He took it outside, where the sky had remained grey, and across the courtyard to the laundry. After dropping it into the clothes basket, he stood for a while on the bare concrete floor, then turned on the light.

Inside the basket were the clothes that he had worn yesterday.

His hands trembled as he reached for the jeans and pulled them out, sprinkling the floor with sand and bits of dried mud. Not hurrying, moving carefully and deliberately, he reached into the front right pocket.

His fingertips touched a smooth edge of metal. He put his whole hand around it and pulled it out.

A medallion, burnished bronze. *Laura Kavan. First Place, U13 Girls*. And on the other side were a tennis ball and crossed racquets with *Tacker Bay Tennis Association* around the edge.

Clutching this to his chest, he returned to his room and sat on his bed. So he had, had, *had* spoken with her, and everything that she'd said had been true, because now he could feel her all around him.

How long he sat there, holding the medallion, he couldn't have said, but when he became aware of his surroundings there was more light in the window, and a movement, up there, caught his eye.

It was Mudlark, black and white, head tilted thoughtfully, little black eyes sparkling, looking directly at him.

The boy smiled. 'Mudlark.'

They stayed like that for a while, watching one another, then Jim slowly stood up and moved to the cage. The door was up, open.

He lowered it.

'I'll leave food out for you,' he told the bird. 'On my desk. I'll leave my window open at the top, always. We can be friends, if you like. If the other birds attack you, come in here and you'll be safe. But there's no need for you to go back into the cage, ever. You're free now. Free.'

Mudlark could explore the world, and take as long as he wanted, strong in the knowledge that he had this place of safety, this home, if ever he needed it.

So the bird nodded to the boy, and flew off bravely into the morning.